About the Author

Chris Thomasson originally came from Essex but predominantly grew up in Suffolk, where he lives today with his loving family. He enjoys writing stories and combining them with his active imagination, to bring them to life.

Devil's Retribution

Chris Thomasson

Devil's Retribution

Olympia Publishers
London

www.olympiapublishers.com
OLYMPIA PAPERBACK EDITION

A CIP catalogue record for this title is
available from the British Library.

ISBN: 978-1-80074-809-5

This is a work of fiction.
Names, characters, places and incidents originate from the writer's
imagination. Any resemblance to actual persons, living or dead, is
purely coincidental.

First Published in 2023

Olympia Publishers
Tallis House
2 Tallis Street
London
EC4Y 0AB

Printed in Great Britain

Dedication

To my loving family, always with me.

Acknowledgements

Thank you to Val for encouraging me and providing such valued critique and to Tony always on hand to add his support.

Chapter 1

Call to Arms

Waves gently lapped along the soft golden sands of the bay. Rising and falling just as they'd done so for millions of years. Sitting in silence a lone figure soaked in the last of the sun rays, wondering in the natural beauty of the ocean. The beach was eerily empty apart from the gentle sloshing of waves, as he pondered on the events that were about to unfold.

He shivered slightly as nerves and the realisation of what he was to do washed over him. The actions he would take next would not only affect his own outcome, but that all of humankind as well. Settling himself again, he laid down with his hands behind his head, looking up towards the heavens. Breathing slowly and deeply as he waited for the sun to set and for the sign to appear.

The balance between good and evil was tipping once more. In the heavens above, planets were shifting and aligning just as they'd done so every thousand years. He knew his time had come, his chance to save humankind from the clutches of evil and fulfil his destiny. A destiny he'd never even contemplated as possible once. He was now part of an ongoing battle; a battle that had been raging for millennia.

All had been taken from him, his lover, his friends, his wealth, his happiness, but worse, all reality as he knew it. A paradox was in effect, good and evil were once more facing off and he was in the middle of it. Lose and the balance of power would be tipped, allowing evil to rise once more. Taking back what good had held on to for so long. Over millennia, evil had been trying to tip the scales back in their favour. Inflicting disasters, global warming, pandemics, famine, even war in a long string of attempts to take back power.

Over time, humankind had unknowingly helped play its part, becoming desensitised—consumed by its own greed and need for self-wealth and growth—something that evil hadn't even predicted would happen. In celebration of starting to prevail once more, the devil was busy preparing for an onslaught. Jack couldn't let this happen, not now, not after everything he'd suffered. He had to act, he had to be strong, he had to succeed.

He watched the clouds as they slowly drifted past in the sky above. Pondering sleepily on the previous day's activities that had led him to this moment and for what lay ahead. He closed his eyes, thinking about the earlier twenty-four hours and gently fell asleep.

The previous day had been spent running through final preparations in the monastery. The high priest had led him to the library where hundreds of ancient books and scrolls were stored. The two copies of the Garima Gospels were already placed on a double rehgal stand ready to be read. One held open on a precise page weighted by a gold book-mark on a slim gold chain that joined to the stand, and he began to speak.

"Ethical justice my son, veers between the notion of forgiveness and retribution. Punishment is a form of justice inflicted as vengeance for a wrong-doing or seeking retribution," the high priest advised.

"The question being, is it right to seek vengeance for a wrong-doing and to what extent. Law and justice as we know is used as the balance between right and wrong and whichever way the scales tip is a means to an end. In modern times this is the difference between freedom or imprisonment. In ancient times it meant the difference between life or death itself."

He carried on looking at the ancient text as he continued with his lesson. "However, if vengeance is sought via other means, revenge for example, the balance of scale tips. From good it moves towards evil, starting a path that then only leads to darkness. Is it therefore right to seek vengeance in this form and if so what if death becomes us as a result. What happens to the victim's soul and in turn what becomes of the soul of the life taker, do they both ultimately fall into the ownership of the devil?"

He lifted the bookmark and turned the page before continuing.

"One thing is for certain, hunter, a level playing field exists that cannot be changed. The certainty of life and death itself, although death is a given what can be forged and manipulated, is the timing and manner of it. Death by natural causes being the given, but if untimely or suspicious an unbalance occurs. The soul instead of finding a path to the heavens becomes lost. Left roaming between the present and the past for ever. If intercepted, it will then be used to feed the devil and its demons. In turn the soul of the lifetaker becomes doomed and their fate? the devil takes them, turning them into demons, forced to serve it for the rest of eternity."

Turning the other book, he read the ancient script in front of him, translating from Latin to English. "The words of the sins my son":

1. "Gula- (gluttony)"
2. "Luxuria/Fornicatio- (lust/fornication)"

3. "Avaritia- (avarice/greed)"
4. "Superbia- (pride/ hubris)"
5. "Tristitia- (sorrow/despair)"
6. "Ira- (wrath)"
7. "Vanagloria- (vainglory)"

"Breaking any of the sin's sets you on a path that only leads to evil, eventually ending with the destruction of the soul. Break them all and the devil will unleash its ultimate punishment on you- Retribution!"

He continued to read out loud, "Retribution, comes in many forms- punishment, justice, reckoning, revenge, payback - all of which you have already fallen foul of, when the devil was manipulating you."

He now chose another book, removing it from a lower shelf and walked around the room translating the late middle English text.

RET- RIB-UT-ION
"RET"
"**Ret**: Past particle, Soak (flax or hemp) in water to soften it… the flax has been retted and used as linen to produce the fabric… the late middle English translation- **to rot**"
"RIB"
"**Rib**, Old English verb dating from the mid-16th century; the sense 'tease' was originally a slang meaning-**to fool, dupe**"
"UT"
"**Ut:** Its definition, Universal Time, **never ending**"
"ION"
"**Ion**: Denoting a resulting state or product- **Oblivion**"

"These are all codes for one thing and one thing only…

14

evil... there is however an eighth unwritten Sin my son and this being?"

"Distraction?" responded Jack.

"Good, remember you must keep calm and trust all your senses when you face evil. The Devil will use any distraction and means possible in its arsenal to weaken and over-power you. The Devil wants to claim its throne on the upper earth once more... the devil wants retribution."

He stared at Jack sternly. "Remember the teachings you received and how the devil came to be and how Christ was overthrown. We cannot allow evil to reign over this land once more, you are humankind's only hope."

Putting the books away, the high priest led the way to the arms room where all antiquities were stored. Ancient weapons used for the sole purpose of destroying evil. Evil that was gaining strength and momentum, inflicting itself on the world once more, a world that had lost touch with itself.

A seventieth Century German crossbow was handed over, wrapped in goat skin leathers along with two long ancient looking, tapered nails. Their forged square ends leading down to sharp points, each one having the slightest of curves near their tips.

"When the time comes, you will meet the keeper who'll provide you further items to help protect your passage into the devil's realm. You have been trained in the use of and understand the importance of the antiquities and all that they stand for, so you must not allow the devil to capture them."

"I understand what is to be done master," said Jack as they walked to the end of the room and through another door.

"You're to wait at the oceans edge tomorrow and as sundown arrives, you will receive the sign to stand and take up arms."

"Is that all I'll have to fight with, the crossbow?"

"No, my son, there are other artefacts that can be used. The keeper will have these ready for you when you meet."

"Are you sure it'll be tomorrow night, master and how will I know who the keeper is?"

"All will become clear, my son, the planets are aligning as predicted from the ancient readings. You have all you need from me, there is nothing further to discuss in here."

Leaving the arms room, the pair headed to the Golden Chamber to see final preparations. The chamber had stood below the castle for over a thousand years. A huge room with a vast vaulted ceiling, supported by full height columns and archways. Everything inside was coated in gold leaf, which looked beautiful in the dim light. Under the ceiling itself, a reflection of the cosmos was on view, mysteriously floating in the air above them. Planets could be seen, slowly moving, and spinning showing an event happening in the universe.

The main altar sat at the top of a small set of stone steps, large enough for a group to stand or kneel at. To the side hung a life size crucifix with a golden statue in the form of Christ set in it, looking down sad and forlorn.

Around the altar and main chamber, large candles lit the vast expanse, dripping wax down their tall mounts. The wax which had built up over hundreds of years, then spreading down to the floor. Incense set in golden globes, hung from chains waved around as young priests walked the floor area. Spreading the smoky aroma around as they waved them.

In the floor itself, white grooves marked out a large compass, set around a central globe shape. The segments then pointing just like a compass, North, South, East, and West with smaller segments pointing Northeast, Northwest, Southeast, Southwest.

Around the chambers perimeter eight Black doors were fixed and aligned to each compass point. Between the doors and the compass, a deeper wider groove fed from the central globe, providing a direct connection to each one. The doors themselves led nowhere, just the old masonry walls of the chamber behind where they were fixed. Jack wondered what their importance was as the high priest addressed the portal guardians and monks, that had gathered with them.

"Tomorrow, the chosen brothers you see before you will take their place in the inner circle, ready to be called upon to assist the hunter." The guardians themselves then kneeling by the altar ready to be blessed by the high priest.

The rest of the monks congregated in a mix of prayer and meditation while younger monks continued their preparations. As one process completed, so the next began in the same manner as incense were swayed around. Prayer, meditation, followed by preparation, then more prayer. Under Christ's statue a large black cauldron sat slowly filling. Droplets of water flowing from its eyes and down its body, before feeding into a trough connected to the cauldron.

The high priest now turned to face Jack directly. "For now, I can share no more with you my son, it is time for you to leave this place."

Gathering the crossbow and nails, Jack was then led back to the chambers main doors and shown out. Leaving the monks to continue their own preparations alone. Tucking the leather goat's skin under his arm, he made his way back through the monastery towards the ancient winding staircase. From there he made his way up to the church above and waited at the back for the public to leave. As the last of them left, he started making his way through the mount's main public areas and down to the causeway.

Stopping midway he looked back to see the high priest watching. He nodded respectfully, placed his hands behind his back and turned to head back towards the church. Jack carried on across the causeway back to the mainland and headed off to where his Range Rover was stored. Driving through the night, he made his way northwards, before turning East and heading towards the coast. It was early afternoon when he finally arrived and tired from his journey, settled himself on the beach to wait. Soaking in the afternoon sun, he listened to the waves as they gently washed up against the shore and closed his eyes.

Slowly waking again, he could hear the noise of the waves breaking and the soft kiss of the summer breeze on his face. Sitting up and checking his watch, he was shocked to see it would soon be sunset. Exhausted from the previous days preparations and the journey he'd been asleep for hours.

'Will the sign appear tonight and what do I look for,' he said to himself? 'Were the ancient predictions correct, can I fulfil the burden placed on my shoulders,' his mind was in over—drive as he became fully alert again.

In the Golden Chamber the guardians removed their brown robes to reveal linen battle clothing. A mix of white outfits, with a blend of orange and white tops. The high priest then taking his position in the centre of the compass, as they knelt at each compass point facing towards the black doors.

The portal Guardians dressed in white Cossacks faced North, South, East, and West while the others, dressed in white and orange Cossacks faced the North-East, North-West, South-East and South-West doors. Each had a small array of weapons laid out next to them. A combination of vials of holy water, curved daggers and fighting sticks—all designed for close contact fighting.

Other monks now gathered, positioning themselves outside the compass. Joining them in prayer as the high priest released the valve at the bottom of the cauldron. Christ's tears then released, filling the groves in the floor, trapping the guardians and the high priest inside. Addressed his band of chosen brothers, he stood tall with his staff raised aloft.

"Remember guardians when a door turns red a portal will open. Our sole purpose is to protect it for as long as possible, giving the hunter time to return. If he fails, reclaiming the antiquities will become your main priority. They cannot fall into the hands of the devil... Good luck my brothers in a few hours our calling will come."

On the beach Jack sat waiting for the sign not really knowing what to expect as the sun began to slowly sink. He stood up and impatiently stared out at the ocean as it began kissing the top of the water. 'It's not going to happen, the high priest got it wrong,' he thought to himself in frustration. Yet as it disappeared below the water line, a bright blue flash occurred, spreading quickly landwards towards him.

Just as it hit, a strong gust of wind pushed him slightly off balance bathing him in blue light. Holding his arms out to help balance himself, his hair and clothes rustled violently before it disappeared. The sign had come, and he knew it was time to take up arms.

Making his way back up the beach, he headed to the car park to his Range Rover and got in. Sitting for a short while, he reflected on the life he used to have as he gripped the steering wheel. Then touching his necklace, he asked it to heal him if he were to become injured and started the engine. With one last look in his wing mirror, he drove off into the early evening heading for the warehouses where his destiny awaited.

Chapter 2

Destiny Awaits

Turning into the alleyway at the warehouse's, a white limousine slowed. Flashing its lights into the darkness to signal its arrival, before slowly moving forwards again. As it drew level with one of the buildings, a robed figure appeared from the shadows. Trying to see into the back through a half open rear window, before sinking back. A pair of red eyes then stared at him from inside as it drove past, and the window shut again.

A curtain of pure energy parted like waves as it slowly drove through into the darkness beyond. The figure then reappeared, trying to follow before it resealed, only to be bounced off as he reached it. Putting his hands on the energy force, he pushed hard. Managing to push it inwards, only for it to deflect again, as if he were pushing against a bubble that wouldn't burst.

Demons guarding the other side hissed and spat at him as he tried to break through. "You do not pass this way today," they mocked, "your time will come." Prodding at the wall of energy with their prongs warning him off. Accepting defeat, he retreated to the safety of the streetlights and lowered his hood. Reaching into his robes he pulled out a cell phone and pushed the button to call the pre-programmed number.

A car radio was suddenly interrupted as a cell phone sprung into life, vibrating in the cup holder of the arm rest. Pushing the call accept button on the console, a voice came through the car's speakers.

"He has arrived my brother."

"Is she with him?"

"I am unsure, the windows of the limousine were blacked out with only a rear one slightly open. I could see someone else in the back with him, but I couldn't tell if it was her, I'm not totally sure sorry."

There was silence for a few seconds, as Jack contemplated the situation and sighed deeply. After all they'd been through, he still couldn't believe she'd given in to temptation and betrayed him.

"Okay, John, thanks for the update, I'll be there soon. I'm about an hour away, is the keeper with you?"

"Yes, my brother."

Ending the call, the radio burst back into life and Jack started to reminisce about his lost love. The fun and happiness they'd shared together prior to the devil seducing her. Happy thoughts then turning to resentment, then anger. Realising she was now in the hands of the man who'd destroyed everything he had. He calmed his feelings, burying them deep as he gripped his necklace. Its energy glowing to help hide his emotions before turning the radio up to take his mind off things.

Pulling into a space near the alley, he was met by the monk as he opened his boot to take out the wrapped antiquities.

"I'm sorry I couldn't tell you before brother, but I'm the keeper. I couldn't allow you to know this as it would have interfered with our learning and training sessions."

Taken aback slightly Jack responded. "It's fine, John, don't worry about it, nothing surprises me anymore. As the keeper, the high priest advised you'll have some additional weaponry for me that wasn't at the monastery?"

"Yes," pulling a sack from behind a set of waste bins. He started to rummage inside, pulling out an old battered long leather coat and leather brimmed hat. Jack then questioning what he could possibly do with them.

"This coat and hat will protect you from the acid in the demon's spittle. If you go into the realm unprotected their acid will kill you within a matter of seconds."

Next came a belt with five vials attached. "Holy water from the tears of Christ," the monk explained. "When you get to the end of the alley, throw one of these at the floor and a wall of water will appear. It will keep the demons at bay long enough for you to take your shot."

"What's the others for?" he said, holding one in his hand to feel how it fitted.

"The only way to get out once you're in the devil's realm is to open a portal. The Devil was cursed by Christ as he died and as such has a weakness. When the devil is vulnerable eight red doors appear. Portal doorways allowing the devil hunter every chance possible to escape without being destroyed."

"To open one, you must throw a vial of holy water at it. Christ's tears will change the door from red to black opening a portal back to the Golden Chamber. The chamber is the key you see. When you activate a portal door, it turns from black to red in the chamber and opens, the guardians are then able to assist in helping you back through."

"If you fail however, they'll use the portal to recover the antiquities before they can fall into the hands of evil. You must be aware though brother, once you activate one you will only have a few minutes before it closes again. If one closes so you must open another and the guardians will try and assist again."

Jack looked at brother John more intensely as he continued

listening.

"You'll only have four chances to open a portal so choose the doors closest to you to activate. Make your shot count and get out. Once a portal door is activated there is no way of keeping it open and they cannot be opened from within the chamber itself. So, if all four vials are used and the demon's or the devil blocks your path, you will be left there trapped all alone."

"And the revolver?" quizzed Jack picking it up from the lip of the sack, gauging its feel and weight as he held it.

"Oh yes, if the water wall drops and the demons get through, you have six shots to hold them off. This will help you further while you make your escape. The silver bullets will kill them but beware they'll have no effect on the devil, so use them wisely."

He put the belt on first and holstered the gun, then slipped the long leather coat and hat on, giving the brim a flick as he finished. "I feel like Van Helsing in this, good job there's no vampires to kill," he joked but the moment was wasted as the monk scoffed back.

"You're certainly no Van Helsing—he was an exceptional vampire and werewolf killer, but he met his match as a devil hunter. The coat and hat was all that was left once the demons had finished with him, let's hope you fare better?"

The pair slowly walked to the start of the alleyway where a steely silence was in the air. "Remember your training, the devil has already used all seven sins against you. Don't fall foul of the eighth. Distraction will kill you just like all the earlier hunters, make your shot count, get the kill, and get out through one of the portal doors."

They walked to within a few feet of the energy wall and stopped. It shimmered in the darkness as reflected light from the streetlights bounced off its surface. "How do I get through that;

do you know how?"

John nodded. "To enter the devil's realm, you must pass through the energy force protecting it, push through. I tried but was unable to pass, the demons wouldn't allow it."

"That was stupid, you could have been turned, and we would now be battling each other. That was a bad idea, John, it's risky enough that you're here as it is."

"Sorry, your right, it was foolish of me Jack, I wish you all the luck hunter —kill the devil and release us both from this curse, humankind is relying on you to bring back the balance."

Jack nodded, turned, and walked towards the realms entrance with the crossbow in his arms. As he got close, he could see the energy field in more detail and something behind. Demons shimmering against the energy field's haze, staring back at him. He pulled the collar up on his long coat, to protect his neck and ears and stowed the crossbow inside his coat. Placing both his palms on the energy field, he pushed, and it started to move inwards.

It bowed like a bubble and pushing harder, he watched wide eyed as his hands and lower arms disappeared. A second later re-appearing on the other side, shimmering against the haze beyond. He pushed even harder, and the rest of his body started to go through, until he fully re-emerged on the other side. The monk could now see him in the devil's realm shimmering against the energy field that separated them. "Good luck brother," he whispered under his breath as he pulled back to the shadows to wait for events to unfold.

The heat and stench in the realm were intense, initially making him struggle to breathe properly. The floor and walls of the back alley covered in a warm slimy substance. Almost alien-looking with steam randomly rising in the shimmering heat. He noticed red, and yellow eyes starting to appear from both sides, then hissing and spitting. 'Demons,' he said to himself, walking past as they clung to the walls glaring menacingly at him.

Glancing back, he could see more coming out of the darkness. Communicating with strange hyena like noises almost as though they were hunting in a pack. The spitting and hissing then worsened as he continued, making him feel nervous and vulnerable. Before long he could see a light against the haze in the distance.

Instinctively he knew to head for it and quickened his pace as the smell of burning leather began to intensify. The acid from the demon's spittle now attacking his coat and hat, reminding him time was short. His breathing quickened as the shimmering light got closer and his adrenalin started to kick in.

Creatures were now picking at his coat and boots, bony fingers with sharp claws trying to get a hold. Desperately trying to prevent him from moving forwards and bring him down. Without stopping to glance back, he sprinted to the end of the alley, opened his coat, and threw a vial of water at the ground behind him.

A huge wall of water arose, supplying a welcomed protective barrier, instantly vaporising demons as they touched it. Throwing his coat and hat off, they lay in a crumpled heap on the ground, smoking and steaming. The acid from the demon's spittle had indeed been intense but they'd done their job and now he was past them.

Standing at the edge of a large square, he was surrounded by what could only be buildings in the other realm. Shimmering against the atmosphere of the devil's own realm. Focusing on his surroundings he saw a couple of large waste skips. Various stacks of boxes and a metal staircase that seemed to have half morphed between both realms. A long wall ran along the back with what looked like red doors set in it. Quickly counting them he could only make out six, 'the other two, must be hidden he thought to himself.'

His concentration then interrupted by the sound of music playing and moans of pleasure. The limousine was parked in the middle of the square with its doors open and operatic music playing loudly. Straining his eyes to get a better focus he could see two bodies writhing on its bonnet. His beloved fiancé Leila was making love to the man that had taken everything from him. He was devasted to see she was thère, and calmness was soon lost as rage took over.

"LUCIFER," he shouted as he watched him thrusting, twisting, and writhing snake like with her. Leila screaming with pleasure as he stared back with the look of pure evil in his eyes. Jack shouted again, "YOU BASTARD, IT'S TIME TO FINISH THIS!" pulling the crossbow up to take aim but he'd not loaded it.

Lucifer had already outwitted him; his distraction had worked all too easily. Jack's nerves had taken control and the necklaces power was no longer able to hide his fear. Pulling two pistols out from beneath Leila, he ran one of the shafts down the length of her body as she screamed with pleasure again. "WOOO," he shouted firing off a round into the air with his other gun.

Jack's rage built as he took one of the nails from his belt and loaded it. "Get away from her, she's just an innocent party intoxicated by your evil." Lucifer stopped, casually zipped his trousers back up and stood at the front of the bonnet. Pointing one of his guns at her head he shouted back, "Again what was once yours is now mine, it's so easy to take from you. Like taking candy from a baby." As he pulled the trigger, leaving her motionless across the bonnet before pushing her off.

'Noooooo!' cried Jack firing the crossbow, hitting Lucifer but missed his heart. He fell back against the limousine, then started firing both pistols as he crawled behind for cover. Jack ran for cover himself, to re-load behind the skips but in the heat of the moment, dropped the second nail. Without thinking, he pulled his own revolver. Shooting off three silver bullets, which simply fell straight to the floor as they hit.

Lucifer now began to writhe and twist, transforming into a huge demonic beast. As the transformation completed, he picked the limousine up and threw it at the skips where Jack was hiding. Sliding away they left him fully exposed, and the second nail was now nowhere to be seen, as panic set in. He threw a vial at one of the doors, but it fell short exploding on the ground, the contents disappearing in a cloud of steam.

The beast was now stood holding a whip, which spat out lightening strands as he whipped it backwards and forwards. Jack fired two more silver bullets which enraged the beast further as it ripped the metal staircase from its housing—throwing it across the yard. For a brief second a hole appeared between the two realms, and he could see a way out before it vanished. Reminding him there was only one way out, through the portal doors.

He threw another vial at a door near the water wall, turning it from red to black opening a gateway. On the other side, he could see guardians knelt ready to spring into action from within the golden chamber itself. The high priest pointing towards the North side of the compass, ordering them to be ready.

Running for the portal, he dived to try and get through but with a crack of his whip, the beast wrapped the lightning strands around his ankles, pulling him back to the middle of the square.

The portal then shutting leaving him trapped again. Panicking he ran again, throwing the third vial at another door where a new portal opened. The South-West compass point now activated in the chamber, and the high priest gave the signal to aid the hunter.

Guardians burst through to do battle with the demons just as the water wall dropped into a small steaming puddle. Now in close combat, they sliced and slashed at the demons as they hissed back. Spitting acid, grabbing, and tearing at flesh with their sharp claws in retaliation.

More vials of holy water were thrown, dissolving demons as they attacked but the guardians were soon overcome. Their sheer numbers and ferocity of acid burned badly. Outnumbered and badly injured, they fled back through as it started to close, leaving Jack trapped once more.

"Be ready guardians," ordered the high priest as swung his staff round and round, making the water surrounding the compass run faster. "He only has one vial left; we must be ready to protect the portal when it opens for as long as we can."

There was still no sign of the nail as he looked around but saw the crossbow laying across the other side of the yard. The beast had also spotted it and was throwing and kicking anything it could to prevent him from getting to it. Battered and hurt he managed to get to the crossbow, only to be flung again as he was picked up and tossed.

Thudding against one of the skips, he lay beaten and bleeding with the crossbow still in his arms. Trying to gather his thoughts he caught sight of the missing nail and picked it up. He had one last chance left, if he could only stand long enough to take aim.

He loaded it, pulled the string back locking it into place and settled his nerves. With one vial left and a red door only a few metres away, he tossed it and a portal started to open. Another group of guardians could be seen, waiting for the high priest's order to rush as he took aim. When with one almighty crack of the whip, a lightning strand hit him in the chest. Sending him one way and the crossbow the other. The guardians were ordered to attack again, spewing through to try and help but were soon cut to shreds with each flick of the devil's whip. With one after another getting torn to shreds, they had no choice but to flee back through.

Finally, alone again, the devil transformed back to his human form behind the skips. Standing up, he ran his hands through his black hair, slicking it back into place. "Wooooooo," he cried shaking his head, "That was fucking awesome." Wiping his mouth on a sleeve of his white designer suit jacket. Jack had somehow managed to stand but could barely walk as he slowly limped towards the portal with the crossbow by his side.

Lucifer found one of his guns and slowly walking towards him tilted his head slightly. Shooting him straight in his injured leg dropping him instantly to the floor. With the portal beginning to close and with no guardians there to help, he was becoming trapped.

Dragging himself along he managed to get to the door where a hand appeared to help pull him through, but Lucifer fired again hitting him in the other leg. With the portal sliding shut, he tried to hold on and drag himself through, but he was too weak, letting go as he lost his grip. Just as the opening was shutting another hand appeared. He held his bloodied hands out again in desperation, thinking he'd be pulled to safety but to no avail. Instead, the crossbow and nail were grabbed leaving him trapped to face his fate alone.

Lucifer menacingly continued to walk towards him, tilting his head slowly from side to side, as he fired again. This time hitting him in the upper arm, then again in the other. Totally helpless, Jack laid against the wall, unable to do anything but stare back waiting his fate.

"Now I know what you're thinking, Jackee boy, have I fired all my rounds, in the confusion I'm not really sure?" Pointing the gun again and pulling the trigger, but the chambers were empty. Jack heaved a heavy sigh of relief for a few seconds, knowing he wasn't dead yet.

The gun was tossed aside and from the back of his suit trousers he pulled out Jack's revolver. "Oh, looky at what I have here," showing him his gun. "I know you fired a load of shots off as well but are there any left?" He opened the barrel and there sat one last silver bullet. "Oh Yeah," he shrieked nodding his head up and down like a wild man.

"Again, what was once yours is now mine," and standing a short distance away, pointed it at his head and squeezed the trigger. As the noise echoed around the square, Jack slid down onto his side motionless, his eyes slowly closing as he fell into unconsciousness.

"Can you hear me... open your eyes... he's still breathing but not really conscious," the medics equipment bleeping loudly as they worked hard trying to save him. One of them stood up to ask questions of the small crowd that had gathered, while the other continued to try and stabilise his life signs.

"Does anyone know what happened here? Does anyone know who this is?"

"Yes," said a voice as john stepped forwards.

"He's my brother, this is Jack... Jack Skye."

"His heartbeat's erratic—he's going into arrest," shouted the other medic from the ground. Quick get the pads on while I try and stem the bleed from his head."

"Okay charging… clear," thump.

"Again… charging… clear," thump.

"It's no good we're losing him, charge again to 200."

"Charging… clear," thump. "It's no good."

"Come on, Jack, don't do this… hang in there, buddy, come on… charge again."

"Charging… clear," thump. His body jolted again but was lifeless.

A hazy glow was all that Jack could now see, the voices in the background became quieter and more slurred. He felt himself slipping, slowly drifting further and further away. Voices becoming dimmer, slower, as his thoughts started to wander. "Can you hearrrrr meeeeeeee." His mind now travelling back to his past as he his necklace tried its hardest to heal him, *bleep, bleep, bleeeeep, bleeeeeeeeeeeeep, bleeeeeeeee,* drifting, drifting until silence.

Chapter 3

3 March 2017
(Three Years Earlier)

At the land and property auction, all eyes were on the sales brochures as groups and individuals crammed into the main auction room. Flicking through the pages and circling the properties that were of interest to them. Jack had been to a few now and despite having his inheritance as collateral he'd never actually gone all the way to secure his first auction win.

Using some of his inheritance, he'd taken courses in business studies and property developing which was a seed that had been sown while undertaking handyman work in France. Although he was self-assured in what was required, he wasn't confident enough in big arenas where other people bid against him.

His nerves always frayed, causing him to pull out at the last-minute. Thinking he wasn't good enough and didn't deserve to win. He'd come so far since his wild days of drugs and crime but his lack of confidence and self-esteem, always seemed to get the better of him. The memories of the ghosts of his past still affecting him.

He felt intimidated by the high-flyers in the main buying arena, his insecurities and paranoia making him feel lesser of a person compared to them. Opting again to stand at the back of the room and watch for a while, taking in everything that was going on. The tight knit groups, the consortiums, the corporates, and the individual professionals. All dressed slick and business like whilst others took on different personas.

Builders looking for quick turn-around potentials, dressed in dusty old work clothes. Couples and singles casually dressed, looking for cheap first-time starter homes. Then the watchers who just seemed to float around soaking in the atmosphere but never really bidding. The same routines being repeated just like all the previous auctions. Brochures thumbed, pages marked, phones ringing and people eyeing up the competition.

The groups were in their usual huddles, murmuring, grunting, and nodding at each other as they discussed their options. Every so often looking up and around before resuming their tight huddles again. Jack called them the grazers as they resembled cattle moving around a farmer's field in herds. Each group also had their own dress codes. The consortiums and corporates dressed in their designer suits and dresses and of course the city slickers dressed to impress, talking loudly on their cell phones trying to make themselves look important.

Some were in groups of two or three while some were on their own. Young and keen trying to make their mark on the world and hungry for success. Most of the time bidding on terrible properties and losing money in the renovation process. Having failed to spot the underlined issues in the brochure photos. Jack nicknamed these the kamikazes as it was all do or die with them.

The builders also moved around in groups of two or three. Loud and brash, swearing as they thumbed through their brochures. Quickly dismissing potential problem properties with a quick "that's shit, move on, or turn the page!" Before winking at each other, circling the page they'd dismissed trying to outsmart the others. Jack for obvious reasons named these the cowboys. Rough and ready looking ready to kick off with each other at any time, just like they did in the old western movies.

Then there were the first time-buyers, flagging up potential lots to bid on. Writing at the top of each page how much their budgets could stretch to. These he called the meerkats as they kept in their little huddles. Always with one scanning the room, looking to see if they were being watched. While the rest continued looking for opportunities hidden between the brochure pages.

As for Jack, he was just trying to get enough courage to win his first auction and secure himself a property to renovate. Casually dressed so he was reasonably unnoticeable, he set about the brochure looking for any potential bargains. This time determined his nerves wouldn't get the better of him. Previous attempts had ended in him losing good buys, when he couldn't handle the pressure of bidding against others. His nerves and paranoia a long-standing issue from his childhood, despite the therapy received over the years. In serious settings he would still simply fall apart.

The auctioneer took to the stand addressing the crowd, thanking them for coming to the auction and started the proceedings. Following a brief description of lot 1 he opened the bids to the room. After a few minutes the lot was sold and in a blink of an eye Lot 2 was underway and quickly sold. The lots now came and went in quick succession with buy after buy quickly happening.

The consortiums buying hard celebrating every sale secured with a whoop and high fives. Other individuals acknowledged their wins with a nod, or a discrete waste height fist thrust. The builders were also buying well, securing several dilapidated properties that only they would be mad enough to take on and even the first time-buyers were winning a few bids.

Before he knew it Lot 20 was coming around Jack wanted to make sure this was going to be his. It caught his eye from the moment he saw it in the brochure. The auctioneer started, "lot 20 then is a four bedroomed detached property set in an acre of ground within an area of outstanding natural beauty. Who'll start me at £200,000?"

There was silence in the room Jack was going hot and cold in anticipation as nerves started kicking in. A paddle was raised from a group in the middle, a consortium of half a dozen huddled together nodding and mumbling to each other.

"£200,000 I'm bid who will offer 210?"

Another paddle was raised this time by an individual buyer and the bidding war commenced. The bids quickly rose as the price rocketed fast to £250,000. Jack's maximum budget was £300,000 and the bids were still rapidly rising.

"£285,000 I'm now bid, anymore in the room?" As a bid came in via the internet.

"£290,000 is now bid on-line do I hear anymore?" The room was silent.

This was his moment, with his heart pounding, his body sweating profusely he raised his paddle. "We have a new bidder at £295,000 at the back," said the auctioneer as he checked his screen, but there were no further bids from the internet.

"We're still in the room then at £295,000 anymore?" Again, there was silence. Jack thought he'd done it his heart was pounding with excitement.

The auctioneer viewed the room again before speaking.

"Going once then at £295,000," looking around the room again and checking his screen.

"Going twice," Jack was thinking in his head, 'Yes, Go on.'

But then, "I now have a new bid of £305,000 from the internet, any more offers from the floor?"

He couldn't believe it, after facing his fears and plucking up the courage to finally bid all the way, he was going to lose, his budget exceeded. Then in a moment of recklessness he bid again, this time shouting out "£307,000", this was his full and final offer he couldn't stretch any further.

"Any more then are you all done now?" asked the auctioneer. The room was silent once more.

"Lot 25 then for £307,000, going once."

'Oh my god,' Jack thought, 'Yes this is it it's mine.'

"Going twice."

'Yes, come on, come on,' and as the auctioneer lifted his gavel for the last time he stopped. Looking up from his screen announced, "I now have a new bid of £310,000 offered online, do I hear any more from the room?"

Jack Shook his head he was done he was dejected and frustrated. His visions of becoming a property developer were fading away even before they'd started.

"Lot 25 for a total of £310,000 for the very last time."

"Going once."

"Going twice," and as the gavel was about to fall for the third and final time a paddle was raised in the room causing the auctioneer to stop short again.

"£315,000," came a nervous squeaky voice. There were gasps in the room as people turned to see who the maverick bidder was. Standing red faced and slightly embarrassed was Jack, holding his paddle aloft. The next few anxious seconds seemed to take forever before the hammer finally fell and the property was his. Everyone clapped as he stood excited and proud of winning his first ever lot. The problem now being how was he going to cover the additional £15,0000.

With only a month to complete on the sale, he had to work fast. After maxing out two of his credit cards and securing a small loan, he was able to gather the remaining £15,000 and the deeds were finally his. The property was in a better state than anticipated. The works required mainly being cosmetic rather than structural. He undertook most of the work himself as he'd worked as a handyman in France previously, but it was still a tall order. Slaving for the next three months and borrowing a further £10,000 to complete the renovation, the day finally came when it was ready for resale.

Luck was now on his side and as soon as the property was marketed, a string of eager viewers booked appointments with the estate agent. Amazingly it sold on the first day to a mortgage free buyer for the full asking price of £550,000. The sale was a triumph and after paying off his debts he had money in the bank and there was no stopping him.

Over the course of the next year his property acquisitions grew—he soon had a solid property portfolio and good reputation to go with it. Letting and managing his own stock had gained a lot of respect with other developers; he was now a dab hand at spotting good opportunities, even when others couldn't see what he could. Always grounded, but also driven by the dream of one day securing a big deal. To then move onto his own land acquisitions and private developments.

He also sometimes worked with others, doubling up on investments to help smaller start up groups. So, they could purchase their own properties, sharing the profit returns in the process. People were now paying a freelance premium for his services as well. To find them good opportunities to develop into business ventures like, health spars, conference centres, mini hotels, and restaurants.

The only luxury he afforded himself was a brand-new Black Range Rover that he paid cash for. From a young age he'd always wanted one and went for the most expensive one in the show room. His other luxury was a penthouse flat that he had a mortgage on. Buying it when the balcony reminded him of his time in France and the Gite he'd lived in.

He was a world away from the life he previously had where he was wild and reckless. Spiralling out of control into a world fuelled by drugs and crime. A tormented life where the memories and demons of his childhood ruled everything he did, as if he was being manipulated by a darker force.

A life where his mind was turned into a world of paranoia and insecurity, causing him to even doubt his own sanity at times. Leading him down a path of darkness before finally escaping and running away to find himself.

With his newfound success he also found his nervousness was gone. Soon he was making lots of friends and had become quite popular. Invited to all the lavish parties and best social events in the area. Yet despite his success he felt empty, like he was born for something different not this. There was a yearning to find his true destiny, but he had no idea what it was or where to begin. One constant remained from when he was young however, he always felt the feeling that he was being watched.

At all the lavish parties and events, he would often spot a figure watching him in the background—a skinny, wiry character with slicked back black hair, always wearing designer suits. He would feel a presence and turn to see him watching. Almost appearing from nowhere, unnoticed by anyone else before disappearing again. He couldn't work out if his mind was hallucinating again or whether it was a real person, that just simply blended back in with the crowd unnoticed.

Now financially self-sufficient he started to think about undertaking his own land acquisitions and developments. Firstly though, there were still some good opportunities to be made before taking the final plunge. Many auctions followed, some providing good investment returns and some not so good. The problem for him now was everyone bidding on the same lots he was, thinking he had the inside track on them. This resulted in some careless purchasing, which ate into his profits and finances. This however was all part of the learning curve, and he fully understood the road to success wouldn't be a smooth one.

Choosing to steer away from internet bidding, he preferred the personal approach. Feeling and soaking in the atmosphere of the auction rooms themselves. Learning from his mistakes he switched back to his old tact of keeping to the back of the room or waiting until a lot was about to complete, before coming in at the death to out-bid the competition.

His interest had also started to move towards several larger auctions that were coming up. Including one where several old warehouses were going to be on offer towards the end of the year. If he could get this right, he could turn his dream into a reality. He knew he'd have to sell his own portfolio to raise the capital required as a holding deposit, but it would be worth it. He just needed to find an investor willing to pay the remaining balance within the four-week period to secure the sale. If he couldn't he risked losing his money which would then leave him bankrupt.

Any spare time he had was spent researching them, looking for any information on their history, construction and what he could do with them. Weighing up how far he was prepared to go financially without over committing and putting himself at risk. Often working late into the night looking at different options.

Demolish the warehouses and build on the land, renovate, and turn them into luxury flats or simply buy and quickly sell on for a higher price to a larger company.

In the meantime, more smaller auctions came along. With one having some particularly good properties on offer. He had a hard copy of the brochure and picked out four lots to go after. This time he chose to arrive for the start rather than arrive at the last minute. Standing to one side watching as the room started to fill. All the usual suspects were there, undertaking their same predictable routines. Waiting for the start when the auction room doors burst open, admitting a new group who marched in loud and obnoxious.

The leader was tall and wiry with slicked back black hair. Wearing a white designer suit and holding a walking cane with a silver skull on top. He pointed around the room with bony fingers, nodding as he marched through the crowd. Intimidating people as he went, staring hard into their eyes, almost looking into their very souls. Pushing his way through until finally reaching the middle where he stopped. There were rumbles and moans of discontent from all around as he took prime position. But the mystery man loved every second his sheer arrogance overbearing the crowd.

Jack recognised him straight away, he was the figure he'd seen at some of the recent parties. Just staring at him inquisitively before suddenly vanishing. He also recognised Jack straight away and walked over to where he stood. "Ah… Jack, isn't it?" Tilting his head to one side slightly, staring hard into his eyes. "Jack Skye or should I say Jack Johnson? it's hard to tell who you really are?" Tilting his head, the other way trying to gauge a reaction.

The Shock his original identity was known, took him off

guard and nerves pulsed through his body once more, as though they'd never left him. "And you are?" was all he could muster as a response.

"Who am I indeed, I am because I am, I am because I can and I'm everything that you're not," he replied mockingly.

He stared hard at Jack's face again, inquisitively tilting his head from side to side in an intimidating manner. Jack having no reply simply looked down at his brochure, wishing he would go away. Bored at getting no reaction the mystery man eventually skipped back over to his group, grabbing a brochure from his assistant.

The auction commenced and as usual the lots were going quickly. Jack could feel eyes burning into the back of his head which was unnerving him. He failed to bag the first three of the lots he was after as a result. Leaving the room for a few minutes to recompose himself, he walked back in, this time choosing to stay at the back.

His fourth potential lot was coming up and he badly wanted it. He'd already lost out on the others and the potential loss of profit was hurting him. The bidding started and the offers swiftly rose. Other bidders thought he had the inside track on another good property and wanted it for themselves. quickly coming to his limit, he stopped, to try and slow the bidding down. Interest then slowed as people realised, he wasn't bidding anymore. As the hammer was about to fall on a bid from another party, he took his opportunity to counter.

His bid was bettered again by the other party, and it was now a tussle just between the two of them. He pushed his bid up by another £5000 and the other party shook their heads showing they were no longer interested. He waited nervously as the auctioneer stood poised ready with his gavel when a loud voice called out.

"This is all very tedious isn't it, I thought it'd be much more fun. Come on people let's spice it up a bit, shall we? Auctioneer I raise the bid by another £25,000." The mystery man was almost bouncing on the spot as he wiped saliva from his mouth across one of his designer suits sleeves.

"Your bid Jackee boy." Teasing him as he looked across at the new bidder. Jack was worried, he looked quite wild and smiled in an evil sarcastic manner. He was seriously outbid and completely unnerved as he shook his head, indicating he was out. The auctioneer banged the top of his podium with the gavel as the words "Sold to the gentleman in the white suit," rang out.

"Your name please sir, if you don't mind you have no paddle."

"My name… oh, yes of course, my name is Lucifer."

"And your last name please?" As the auctioneer wrote in his journal to record the sale.

"Diablo." Nodding smugly as he looked around the room. Slowly turning in a circle, holding his walking stick and arms up.

For the rest of the auction Jack kept outside as Lucifer continued to buy up everything that came up. Seriously out bidding anyone who tried to go against him. Money seemed to be no object to him, he was both arrogant and frivolous. Jack took himself for a walk to calm himself down. Walking along he tried to work out what had just happened. 'Who is this guy and what's he all about?' he kept saying to himself. 'If he can outbid me just like that, he could ruin me.' He really needed to find a serious backer if he wanted to stand any chance of winning the warehouses. Especially if this new guy was going to stay around.

The auction ended and Jack stood by his Range Rover checking his cell phone as Lucifer walked past. "Nice wheels Jack, shame you lost, but get used to it, I'm going nowhere," as he made his way to a white chauffeur driven limousine. Jack just stared at him rather than respond, they'd only just met, and he already despised him. He then heard a whistle; Lucifer was waving at him to get his attention again. As he went to get in the back of his limousine, he shouted across. "What was briefly yours is now mine," he scoffed arrogantly before shutting the rear passenger door.

As the limousine pulled alongside, it slowed and a rear window opened, Lucifer was busy snorting cocaine. Using a long fingernail on his right-hand to scoop it up to his nose where he sniffed hard. He shook his head wildly and stared hard at Jack, yelling "Yeahhhhhhhhh," before flicking his wrist to indicate for the chauffer to move on.

Jack's drive home was torturous, the thoughts of what this man could do running around and around his head. He couldn't afford to lose everything he'd planned and worked for. He needed a backer and a plan if he was going to be a contender. This new-comer could ruin everything for him.

Later that evening he sat looking at the photograph of his parents and brother, smiling at them as he touched their faces with his fingers. He put the frame back on the table and turned to the other one of him as a teenager standing with his grandparents. He sat feeling the frame and touching their faces, remembering their love for him. Even though they were in old age when they were bringing him up, they'd been the closest thing to real parents he'd experienced, following the death of his parents.

He thought about his younger days, growing up and the places they visited and explored together. Innocent fun days, before getting himself into drugs and trouble. His rebellion against the betrayal he'd felt towards his parents. Spending all their time with his older brother when he was ill, leaving him in the care of his grandparents. The resentment then pushing and leading him down a path of self-destruction and darkness. He remembered his troubles as a young adult, how out of control and reckless he'd been. Helplessly manipulated by everything around him as though some other force was driving him. If he'd not left when he did, he would either have been imprisoned or worse be dead by now.

He poured himself another glass of red wine and sat again to ponder. "Alexa, play some Ibiza chill out," he called out and as the music filled his lounge his mind started to drift. The tunes reminding him of his times in Amsterdam and France.

Exhausted from the stress of the day he let his mind wander to the time when he was wild and out of control. He continued to run his fingers around his grandparents faces as memories of those dark times came flooding back.

Chapter 4

28 May 2015

Amsterdam had opened Jack's eyes in more ways than one, he was like a kid in a candy store. For a guy in his early twenties everything it had to offer was all too tempting. His first experience was watching the junkies hanging around one of the many canal bridges just before daybreak, waiting for their next drugs fixes. They were skinny hunched over and forlorn, almost soulless with sunken red and yellow eyes. They looked demonic in appearance, shaking and desperate for their next hit.

From the bridge's underside, red eyes peered out of the darkness. Almost belonging to strange creatures that seemed to cling to the walls. Every so often, blue flashes were seen, striking out almost like lightning in the darkness. The sound of screams ringing out followed by silence.

As with every visit, their trip started at their favourite coffee shop on the other side of one of the canal bridges. It always opened early, ready to greet the ferry passengers that had docked before dawn. The gang would have a coffee while choosing what drugs to buy and they'd laugh and tease each other about their previous visits.

Jack ribbed one of his friends reminding him of when they first visited the red-light district. How he'd bragged he was going to have as many prostitutes as he could, only to bottle his nerve standing in front of the very first window, too scared to go in.

Jack then pushing him aside and walking straight in to have his first encounter.

The rest of the group burst out laughing as they joked how they egged him on while Jack was inside having fun. Until eventually, he nervously made his way to the next window and slowly walked through the door. Smithy reminded them how Mike had then appeared back outside before Jack had finished. How they cheered as the prostitute held up her little finger as she sat back at the window, indicating he had a tiny knob. Everyone howled with laughter as Mike turned bright red, telling them all to "Fuck off."

The coffee shop had a Rastafarian theme and Reggae music thumped out all day with huge speakers set up on the outside. The shop had a floor mounted presentation cabinet, just like in a sweet shop only it was drugs that were for sale. The only confectionary on offer being small sponge delights, with magic mushrooms or small lumps of dope inside instead. Behind the counter shelves were set against multi coloured walls. Taking pride of place was a bong, shaped like a human a skull, fitted with half a dozen pipe attachments.

The café owner always greeted the group with a big smile and open arms. Puffing on a huge joint that never seemed to leave his lips. The group always sat at their favourite table, a corner booth away from prying eyes and ears. The bench seating laid out in an 'L' shape in the corner, which was cushioned with burgundy-coloured coverings against green walls.

The owner would ceremonially place the bong in the middle of the table and the gang would start. Getting totally stoned before spending the rest of the day sampling the sights and delights that Amsterdam had to offer. They'd kick off with a trip to the sex museum, watch the naked dancers and a sex show before finally hitting the red-light district.

The gang joked how two of them had once taken a wrong turn in one of the back streets. Only to end up opposite a large building that looked like an old cinema. There were men and women everywhere. It wasn't until two men walked past wearing tight leather trousers with their bums on show, that they realised they were in the wrong area. The gang roared with laughter as they recalled the shock on their faces when they finally made their way back.

Their routine had become synonymous with the group, always drugs, alcohol, prostitutes, and no sleep. This trip however was going to be different and more serious. This time it was about scoring drugs to sell back home—it was business and not pleasure.

Jack though, was wild and reckless; he played hard, he partied hard and didn't care about anything. Seeing and experiencing things that the average person could only dream of. Often bordering on the strange and supernatural, things he just couldn't explain. At times it was as though he was possessed by other forces, driving him to taste the forbidden fruits on offer. Inside he felt alive almost electric, intoxicated by the experiences he'd never tried before. All the time unknowingly being forced down a path leading towards darkness and evil. Seduced and manipulated by the deadly sin's that were taking him there.

In the red-light areas, every street would be filled with people. Prostitutes would sit on their stools in their little shop windows trying to tempt clients in off the streets. Each street becoming more specialised and seedier the deeper you entered, as it catered for all needs and tastes.

Fuelled by cocktails of dope, LSD and alcohol, Jack would stand in front of the windows, choosing which girls to pick. Some girls would dress in red, white, or black dresses while others dressed in sexy lingerie, blowing kisses as people walked past. Their small booths lit by a single red-light as they beckoned with their index fingers for people to come in. He always found it difficult to stare for too long, as the girls almost seemed to morph in and out of normality in front of him. One minute looking stunning, the next hideous almost demonic, as though some force inside was transforming them.

At times it looked like hands were caressing their bodies from under their skin. Moving around groping and squeezing as the girls stared back with red and yellow eyes. Licking their lips with pointy tongues before transforming back into stunning women again. He put this down to hallucinations, the LSD would make him see and hear things that weren't real. Playing with his mind and making him over paranoid. He'd also learned that the drug enabled him to challenge his mind. When heavily hallucinating, he could explore and expand his subconsciousness beyond anything he knew.

Its downside was the paranoia, his mind often playing tricks on him. Often catching glimpses of people, giving the feeling they were following him, watching his every move. The most shocking hallucinations came from staring at his own reflection in front of mirrors. He could almost see his dead brother, sitting in a small basic room. Painted white with no windows, just a small desk and chair, a small single bed and a candle providing light as he sat studying a large old book.

In every vision his brother would then turn, looking shocked before throwing water at him, making the vision disappear. Sometimes he could almost feel the water hitting him and he would wipe his face with his sleeve. Again, he put this down to the drugs playing tricks with his subconscious mind as he knew his brother was dead. He'd died years earlier while being treated for his illness at twelve-years-old.

At the start of his illness, he was kept locked in his bedroom after his parents said he was contagious. Eventually taking him away to get treatment at a specialist centre, leaving Jack in the care of his grandparents. On a visit home one day, his parents were involved in an accident where their car came off the road and they were killed.

The crash investigators found they'd swerved to miss something large, and the car went out of control. Smashing through a barrier and plunging down a slope before exploding as it hit a tree. A few months later he had the sad news that his brother had died while receiving treatment. Leaving Jack to be brought up by his aging grandparents.

He had to grow up quickly as although they loved him like a son; they were too old to bring up another child. Instead, he found solace in groups of friends that then led him on a path of self-destruction. He'd become a known troublemaker and was mixing with the wrong people. Experimenting with anything that would numb the pain of his past as he rebelled. The drugs and alcohol initially starting off as a crutch. Something to take the edge off but now he was older, they were starting to take over his life, he was spiralling out of control.

He reminded himself that this trip was all about scoring drugs to sell back home. He could make some money to then perhaps get away and start afresh somewhere new. He was following the lead from the rest of the group who'd already been sourcing supply from Amsterdam. They were all due to meet up with their supplier later that day.

Jack, however, was already in the red-light area. Looking for a prostitute that had always caught his eye, but he'd never indulged with until now. Forgetting he had a meeting arranged with the others, he stopped as she caught his eye again. Dressed in a white silk dress, she looked stunning with long flowing black hair and brown eyes. She held him in a trance as she slowly moved her hands up and down her body as she sat on her stool. she was spell binding to him and this time her moves enticed him in.

Meeting at the door next to her booth window she gestured to a slim flight of stairs. The wooden stairs rose steeply like a loft ladder and a rope hung to help pull himself up. At the top she led him into a dimly lit small lounge. To the side was small a bedroom, a toilet and a sink set to the side. Although the room was dimly lit, he could see it's neutral colour scheme and the strong smell of sex.

She slowly slipped off her dress to unveil the sexy white lingerie she was wearing against her perfectly formed body.

"What would you like?" she queried.

"To watch," he replied sitting down in a small armchair, crossing his legs, and letting his arms flop either side of the armrests.

"What's your name?" he asked.

"You can call me Angel."

"Ha, does that mean your heaven sent, where's your wings?"

Angel laughed. "I'd hardly say I'm from heaven, you're in a whorehouse after all. Let's just say I'm more like a horny little devil," smiling back at him and tilting her head to one side slightly.

She walked over and gently placed a foot on his lap. Slowly she ran her hands up and down her white stockinged leg, showing off her suspender belt before slowly unclipping it. Then repeated the process with the other, slowly running her fingers up and down before removing it completely. Walking sexily across to the sofa opposite she sat down.

"The price to you will be one hundred and fifty Euros."

He took out his wallet and placed the cash on the side table next to his chair. Then put an elbow on one of the arm rests and supported his chin with his hand. Facing him, she slowly slipped off her thong and reached over, taking what Jack had initially thought was an ornament off a small table next to the sofa. She held the wide base of the vibrator and moaned as she pleasured herself, Jack sat mesmerised as he watched what was going on.

"Would you like to have a go?" she asked looking across at him.

She guided his right hand and encouraged him to slowly explore with it. Over excitedly he was too fast, and she gently held his wrist, advising him to slow down before showing him what to do. Her body then started to morph just like the others had. She suddenly looked like she was being caressed all over from inside her own body. Hands moving around under her skin, caressing and groping as she groaned with pleasure.

The LSD was making hallucinate again and his pupils were wide-eyed. "You like your drugs yes, you're tripping. I can feel you are starting to get hard." As she rubbed the front of his jeans. Standing up she held both his hands and gently led him to the bedroom, gesturing for him to lie down on the bed naked.

Standing above him, she began pleasuring him. "You want to fuck, yes?"

"Yes," he replied as she gently continued.

"You'll have to pay me another one hundred and fifty Euros or if you have more money, I will stay with you all night."

"You have more money? I'll stay with you," she sighed excitedly.

Stopping for a moment she walked over to where his clothes were and rifled through his wallet. "You don't have enough here, no more for you." Walking back over to put on a dressing gown on, before telling him to wash his hands and get dressed. His time was up, and she had other clients waiting outside.

As he cleaned himself, he noticed the pedal bin was full of paper towels and used condoms and he felt disgusted. He got dressed and watched her prepare herself for her next customer, without even giving him a side glance. He washed his hands once more then turned to face her. Asking why she stopped only for her to reply sternly.

"You're just a client. You have no more money. You were given what you had paid for, nothing else."

He didn't understand what was going on, a voice inside his head was telling him to get his money's worth. He felt powerless to stop himself as a force seemed to take over him. He grabbed one of her arms and shook her slightly. "I want my money's worth—you've not satisfied me yet," raising his voice.

"You watched me as requested, you've had what you paid for, now get out." Angel looking concerned, glanced over to a wall where a small panel slid open. She nodded, and a door opened where a bouncer appeared from a corridor behind.

Letting go, he stood looking pathetic against the giant of a man in front of him. "You heard the lady get out or do you want me to evict you?" Jack held up his hands in submission and gestured he wanted no trouble. He headed for the steep staircase when a force hit him from behind and he tumbled to the bottom. Before he could get back onto all fours; he was lifted and flung straight out of the door back onto the main street.

He pulled himself up off the cobbles, brushing himself down as people stared at him in disgust. He looked at the window to see his reflection, he looked almost unrecognisable. Like an evil had taken control of him as his face appeared to transform back to its normal state again. He felt like he'd been had, and he was ashamed of what he'd just done.

Angel had already returned to her window booth and switched the light back on like a taxi waiting for its next fare. He walked off head, held low in disgrace, unsure of what had just happened. He'd completely lost control of his thoughts and actions and was helpless to stop it. He could no longer understand what reality was and he felt like he was starting to lose his sanity.

Catching up with the rest of the group who were already smoking more dope at the coffee shop, he relayed his experience. His good friend Boomer just laughed. "Didn't you know all the whore houses have corridors running behind so that the bouncers can look after the girls on behalf of the pimps?"

"What… really?"

"Yep, probably film it all as well. I wouldn't be surprised if one day we're all on some porno movie with the number of girls we've had in those places. That reminds me I've an appointment with the nymph sisters, I haven't seen them yet this trip. Those two really are filthy little wenches, you should try them sometime," smiling as he got up and left.

Jack explained to the others that he'd lost control of his thoughts and body, unable to stop himself from trying to force himself onto Angel. Through the dense smoke, a vision of a face appeared that looked like pure evil. Almost inhuman that spoke in a deep voice that he hadn't heard before.

"Trouble with you is smoking too much of this shit and mixing it with LSD. It's screwing with your mind," poking his head with a finger as he carried on. "LSD is only for people with strong minds and you're starting to lose yours, Jack. I feel it's time for us to be finally introduced," as it disappeared back into the smoky fog laughing.

"Jack… Jack!" He turned and recognised his friends again. "For fuck's sake why don't you stop taking that shit and start focusing on the deal in hand like the rest of us."

"Is everything all right mate you, okay?" came another voice. "You look like you've just seen the devil or something?"

"Sorry," said Jack, "I… think… I… I really need to give this stuff up. I'm seeing and feeling things now that I've never seen or experienced before. It's messing with my mind; I think I'm losing it."

Micky piped up, "For fuck's sake, you're just tripping your nuts off again, that's all. Here have a puff of this spliff that'll sort you out." Jack took a huge drag and as he exhaled was wasted again, passed-out as he slumped across the table.

Coming around again, it was late afternoon and he found himself laying on a bench overlooking a section of canal. A veil of smoke was around his face as Micky had given him a shotgun. "Here he is, sleeping beauty. Come on," he said in a lively voice. "You missed doing the deal with the supplier's dick head. Time to get back to the train station to see what the others scored."

At the station, the rest of the group hurled abuse and laughed that he'd been too wasted to do a deal. Boomer pulled out an A4 size sheet of blotting paper, covered in small-printed squares with a picture on each on. "Black snakes," he nodded triumphantly. "These little babies will go down a storm back home plus all the E's as well. I'm set to make a bomb." He held the sheet high to show it was soaking wet from the liquid LSD that was on it.

"Right then time to get these in the post." Taking out the rest of the sheets from his satchel and placing them on the bench in front of them. He then pulled out a hand full of birthday cards and envelopes. The sheets of blotting paper were popped inside the cards, home addresses were put on the envelopes and the envelopes sealed. Stamps were then stuck on, and the whole lot posted in a mailbox outside the station. "Happy Birthday boys, it's pay day," he announced.

"Where's the E's then Boomer?" questioned Nick.

"Up my arse mate where they're safe, Don's got a few condoms worth up his as well."

The group boarded the train back to the ferry port and partied like animals on the twelve-hour crossing back. Coming back through customs they went their separate ways, agreeing to meet in a couple of days once their goods had arrived.

A few days later, Jack received a phone call from Micky. "The guys have been caught and are in custody, charged with drug smuggling. They were raided as soon as the postman delivered the cards. the Police had been on to them for months and followed everyone the whole weekend. The only reason we've not been pulled in yet is because we didn't write out any envelopes with our addresses on."

Jack was a mess; he would've been in the cells as well if he'd managed to score, instead of blowing his cash on taking drugs. With no one about to hang around with, he decided this was his break—he needed to escape, to try and find himself and clean himself up. If he stayed, he had no doubt it would go wrong for him. He had to find somewhere cheap but far enough away to disappear for a while unnoticed. Clean his life up and re-find himself.

He consulted with his grandparents who recognised he had problems. Putting it down to the stresses he'd suffered at a young age and the people he'd chosen to hang around with. They agreed he needed to disappear; free himself of drugs and more importantly find himself and rid his mind of his insecurities.

There was a knock at the back door that suddenly interrupted their discussion. While his grandmother went to see who it was, his grandfather sat him down and started talking more seriously to him.

"Whatever happens lad I want you to do me one thing. When you go, don't tell us where you're going. People will ask questions and we don't want to be able to help them." Jack was puzzled as his grandfather leaned forward on his armchair beckoning him to come in closer.

"You're important, Jack, you have a destiny to fulfil. A great burden will be placed on your shoulders one day, but until then you need to stay low and keep safe. The time's not yet right." Jack was even more confused as his grandfather was talking in riddles again.

"Listen lad, there's weird things in this world. Things that you can't contemplate, even in your wildest dreams but in time you will. Whatever you do while you're gone don't contact us, do you understand," putting his hands on his shoulders and shaking him slightly.

"We both love you to death, but we can't put you at any further risk by us knowing where you've gone. Dark forces are around, and they'll try and force us to tell."

"Why?" he asked as he noticed the gold chain around his grandad's neck glow slightly. His grandmother then slowly made her way back into the room supporting herself on her walking stick. They looked at each other, nodding and shaking their heads. Pulling both agonised and surprised expressions as if they were having some sort of telepathic conversation. Then she turned and left the room again.

His grandfather turned back to Jack and grabbed his right

shoulder.

"When you go, you'll be on your own. We cannot be part of what you must do, we cannot help or interfere. Trust no-one and keep moving until you feel safe. Get off this path you're currently on, it will only lead to evil. Free your mind and come back to us a man, ready to face the challenges that lay ahead."

In all the confusion Jack just got more confused and in a fit of anger, stormed out of the house. Jack couldn't sleep at all that night. The thoughts of his friends going to prison, the feeling of being followed all the time and the paranoia he was suffering were all too much. His grandparents were talking in riddles, gold chains were glowing and telepathic conversations. What was going on? was it real or all in his mind? Did the death of his parents and brother have something to do with it all and were his grandparents keeping some sort of secret from him?

The next morning, after his grandparents had left, he headed straight to a travel-agents asking for the cheapest one-way ticket anywhere. There was no rhyme or reason, just a gut feeling to get away as soon as possible. "Anywhere in particular?" asked the travel agent as the screen was turned around showing a map.

He closed his eyes and randomly pointed at the screen and opened them again. "There?" he said.

"Okay let's have a look for you, a one-way ticket to Bordeaux, yes, we can do that. Traveling by ferry from Dover to Calais, picking up a train to Paris for a final connecting fast train to Bordeaux. That will be £250 in total," said the girl as she tapped away at her computer.

"I want to leave tomorrow, is that okay?"

"Sure, no problem," and the ticket was bought.

No-one was home when he got back, so he raided his grandparent's loft for their old two-man tent and some other basics. However, he couldn't find his rucksack, so he had a mad rush back into town to get a new one. After packing he found his passport in the top drawer of the side table, gathered his other things, and left staying overnight in Dover. At the port the next morning he boarded the ferry, blending in with the scores of other passengers that were sailing across. Trying to hide himself as the feeling of being followed was becoming overbearing again.

His paranoia was back, and he was confused. Desperate to escape and break free from the life he was leading. Passing through customs in Calais he caught a train to Paris. Following a short trip on the metro, he boarded a connecting fast train to Bordeaux. From there he would then disappear and try and start putting his life back together.

The journey though was boring and seemed to be dragging on forever. This made his mind race, and his paranoia and hallucinations were suddenly very real and ever present again. Sweating badly and full of anxiety, he could sense people staring at him—was it the police following him wanting to question him, was it the drug suppliers from Amsterdam wanting to take revenge or someone else. He looked out of the window as the train finally pulled into a station and saw a sign saying Bordeaux with a smaller name in brackets next to it.

In a fit of desperation, he grabbed his rucksack thinking he was about to be arrested or worse. Rushed to the carriage door and threw it onto the platform, jumping down himself just as the doors were closing. He then stood on the platform and watched the train until it disappeared into the distance.

Walking out of the station, the realisation hit that he wasn't in the city but a town. Checking his map he saw, there were another three stops to Bordeaux Central station. "You fucking idiot," he shouted out, before noticing a couple of casually dressed gentlemen watching him. Paranoia kicked in again and quickly looking at his map, decided to head for a main road that headed towards Bordeaux. There he could hopefully thumb a lift to the centre of the city, picking up from where he should have got off. He moved fast but as he wasn't used to the full weight of his new rucksack, the straps dug in hard to his shoulders and the pain slowed him down, but he had to keep moving.

Eventually, the noise of flowing traffic could be heard on the other side of an embankment. He'd found the main road, but he was still being followed. The two men kept their distance but were following him. He made his way to the top of the embankment and looked down. 'This isn't a main road,' he said to himself, 'it's a bloody motorway!' Cars flew past bibbing their horns as he made his way down to stand against the side of the motorway trying to move along its edge.

He found a small pull in layby where he set his rucksack down and put his thumb out to hitch a lift. Cars flew past bibbing their horns, but none were going to stop. The two figures had also made they're down the embankment and had started moving along towards him. In desperation he ran out into the motorway waving his arms about, in one last ditch attempt to flag a car down and escape his assailants.

Cars swerved and skidded as they tried to miss him. Blasting their horns as they shot past before an old beaten-up red Peugeot 205 swerved into the layby. Skidding to a halt and throwing dust and stones everywhere as the hand brake was pulled. Jack looked back and his assailants were now starting to run, waving their arms around trying to get him to stop.

"Anglaise," Jack shouted.

"Ah… Anglaise," said the French driver. "Get in," speaking in pigeon-English.

59

Without further ado, Jack threw his rucksack onto the backseat and got in the front. With a huge dusty wheel spin, the car shot off back into the traffic flow. Cars swerved and beeped as he forced his way into the fast lane and put his foot down. His two assailants could be seen in the wing mirror, frantically trying to flag down their own lift, but were soon lost in the distance. The motorway itself coming to an abrupt halt, as cars crashed and skidded in the chaos he'd left behind.

The driver didn't slow down at all but kept his foot flat to the floor weaving in and out of the traffic. Waving his fists and arms around out of his window at cars that wouldn't let him pass. Hurling abuse as he swung from one lane to another while Jack held tight to the dashboard.

"Par… you must be English; no other idiot would hitch hike on a French motorway. where is it you are going?"

"Bordeaux Central," replied Jack.

"I can drop you at the outskirts, it's okay."

Following a half hour white-knuckle ride, they reached the edge of the city. The Peugeot sliding to a stop as the driver hit the brakes and pulled the handbrake at the same time.

"Par these brakes are no good," laughing loudly as they came to a halt. "Friends of yours?" he asked pointing backwards as Jack got out.

"No, they followed me here from England."

"Whatever trouble it is you are in, stick to the back roads, you will disappear there." Jack pulled his rucksack out of the car and with a huge wheel spin, the Frenchman waved his hand out of his window. "Goodbye… crazy fucking English," and shot off in another huge cloud of dust.

It was late when he finally arrived at the closest camp site; six hours of solid walking through Central Bordeaux and into the countryside. With a five stone ruck sack on his back, it was hard work, and he was exhausted. Spending the next couple of days recovering from his ordeal, he started planning his route through France. At least for now he was free, and he could relax a little. By keeping to the smaller country roads, he could also travel at his own pace and lie low.

Chapter 5

Re-finding Himself

On the move again, it was cheap to pitch a tent for only a few Euros a night. If the campsite was nice, he'd stay for a few days or just simply move on if it was uninteresting. He spent the next eight weeks pitching his tent. Slowly walking down through the Loire Valley where the scenery was beautiful. The people were fantastic and welcoming, never questioning what he was doing. He felt great to be away from his old life and the chaos that surrounded it.

He had a feeling of total freedom, an emotion that he'd not experienced before. He was clear of the craving for drugs and the hallucinations and paranoia had all but subsided. With his mind now starting to focus on the future he could finally make a start on rebuilding his life and looking forwards.

He continued his journey heading to Agen, then Montauban, Albi then across to Toulouse. Where he decided to have a few days rest before continuing down to Narbonne and the ocean. He had no idea why he was heading there apart from something inside pulling him. The needs to be at the oceans edge as though to wait for a sign, a calling for him to act.

Finally, after weeks of travelling he arrived. Pitching his tent next to a spit of rocks on the beach, bordering a river inlet. A car park and picnic area was behind, leading off a narrow road and a French camp site sat opposite with showers and toilets. He felt safer by the rocks, away from any risk of being exposed or being found by the authorities.

Life was great, the beach was lovely, the water was fantastic, and the girls were hot, with Jack right in the middle of it. Laying on the rocks soaking up the sun, topping up his tanned body. Despite his newfound freedom there was still a yearning. A burning feeling, he still hadn't found his true purpose in life but had no idea what it was. At night he'd lay on the sand by his small campfire, watching the stars and planets above. Pondering what his future was and what secrets his grandparents had been keeping from him.

Before long two French women in their early twenties started to hang around from the camp site opposite. Initially keeping their distance, just watching and giggling from a distance until eventually joining him by his campfire one evening. A friendship was soon struck and shortly after others joined to exchange stories, play music, and learn more about each other.

Jack always maintaining he was just taking a bit of time out to travel. He didn't want anyone to know he was lying low and never divulged anything about his life back in England. The girls were staying at the campsite for the whole eight-week summer holiday and the camp site was full of other French families enjoying the sun and the sea.

He was told the site had no problem with him using their facilities provided, he was discreet which he agreed. Over the weeks Catherine and Danielle had grown close to him. Spending much of the time hanging around together. He was different sort of cool with a sense of mystery about him which they liked. He was well tanned, had good hair and was toned from all the walking he'd done carrying his rucksack.

Inviting him to swim across the river inlet one hot afternoon, the girls offered to sunbathe on a private section of beach, and he couldn't contain himself. The girls dived in and quickly swam strongly against the current to reach the other side. Jack was fit from all the weeks of hiking but wasn't a strong swimmer. He found the going tough, much to the amusement of the girls who pointed and giggled from the other side.

Catherine had deep tanned olive skin with long flowing black hair and dark eyes. Danielle was blonde and just as beautiful. Both were deeply tanned and wearing matching white bikini bottoms and tight fitting black and blue tee shirts.

Jack was reminded of Angel and how her beauty had stopped him in his tracks in Amsterdam. The girls, knowing he was struggling, stood tantalising him from the other side. Their wet tee shirts sticking tightly to their chests. He was excited and wanted to be there with them but was still fighting the current. Together they lifted their tops, slowly taking them off, teasing him before laying down to soak in the afternoon sun.

Eventually he dragged himself onto the beach, panting with exhaustion. The girls lay giggling as he composed himself again and walked over to join them. As he sat down, they stood up, only to dive back into the water and swim back across the inlet. Giggling loudly as they disappeared over the rocks back towards the campsite. Jack was then left smiling to himself. 'Prick teasers,' he thought to himself as he slowly got back into the water to make the arduous swim back.

Watching the sun rise the next morning, he wondered why the girls had been messing with him. He was frustrated and becoming restless, 'Maybe it's time to move on,' he said to himself. He'd felt the feeling more recently that he was needed back home for some reason. He was in the shower block at six-thirty, which was the best time as it was always empty. He found the unisex showers off putting. Older men and women would walk about naked, with everything sagging and on show. He'd just started to shower when he heard the noise of a toiletry bag being placed on one of the wooden slatted benches next to him.

Facing the wall with his palms against the tiles, he let the water cascade over the back of his head and down his back. He felt a pinch on his bum and turned to see Danielle standing next to him naked. "Bonjour," she said softly lathering her body up under the shower next to him.

"Morning, you're up early." She put a hand on his chest and slid it down his six pack before reaching down. "What is it they say in your country, you have morning glory?"

She moved in close pressing her breasts against his chest gently biting her bottom lip. He lifted her up supporting her weight against the tiled wall, where they slowly made love as the warm water cascaded over them. Afterwards she wrapped herself in her towel and with a wink disappeared again.

That was the last he would see of Danielle, three days later, her car was loaded. Her parents then leading the family convoy out of the camp site to head off back to where they come from. Danielle only slowing to give the briefest of glances to blow a quick kiss as she drove closely behind her parents.

After weeks of rough camping and with money running low, Jack needed to work. He was introduced to a few local farmers and various property owners. Taking on the role of a handyman and managing peoples holiday lets. As a perk he was given a gite to live in while he looked after an old farmhouse owned by a well-off English family.

He spent his time learning how to fix and repair things, sometimes working alongside other French tradesmen as well. Learning their skills and becoming quite good with his hands.

The summer was soon coming to an end and now Danielle had gone, his time spent with Catherine had become almost non-existent. His workload was growing and soon she'd be gone as well, to return to her normal life.

His passion for the stars had also grown, every night scanning the heavens with an old telescope. He'd found it in one of the barns where his Gite was and busily mapped out the cosmos above, using the book that was with it. When he had time, he'd also sit at the oceans edge in the early evening. Just as the sun was setting, almost subconsciously waiting for a sign, a call to do something but he no idea what it meant. He now felt he was born for something more special and began to understand why his grandparents had said he wasn't ready yet.

Coming back one evening after a hard day's work, he noticed the lights were on in his gite. The balcony doors to his bedroom were also open and the linen curtains were flapping in the warm evening breeze. As he got closer, he could see the shadow of someone sitting on the balcony. Walking in he noticed the table had been prepared. A spread of salad and different nibbles were in bowls and mussels ready to be cooked were on the stove. Intrigued by his uninvited guest he made his way upstairs.

He heard a glass being put down on the small balcony table and could the smell perfume. Through the linen curtains he could see a woman sitting, with a bottle of wine chilling in an ice bucket. He watched as she caressed the wine glasses stem and made his way onto the balcony to see who the mystery guest was.

To his surprise it was Catherine, "Bonjour, Jack, I thought I'd come and see you one last time. I haven't seen you for a while and we leave tomorrow. Come and sit with me and have a glass of wine while we watch the sun set."

"Erm, hi Catherine, do you mind if I have a quick shower

first, I stink from working in the hot sun all day. I'll be back in a few minutes."

He made his way to the bathroom and took a Lukewarm shower. Washing the dirt and sweat away before towel drying his hair and putting on a pair of shorts. Unknown to him, Catherine had been watching him getting dry from the position she had on the balcony. She poured a glass of wine and gave it to him as he sat down.

"So, what brings you here then?"

"I wanted to see you one last time and to see if you're okay, you've been so distant lately. I worry about you Jack." He clinked his glass against hers and leaned back in his seat, taking a large mouthful of wine.

They sat in silence as they watched the sun set, only moving when the empty bottle was pushed upside down into the ice bucket. They both stood and walked downstairs to have the meal she'd prepared and sat in deep conversation while their food digested.

Taking another bottle of chilled wine from the fridge they returned to the balcony to watch the stars coming out. "You're fascinated by the stars and planets, what is it about them that holds your attention so much?"

Jack looked over at her. "I'm not sure I've always been drawn to them. It's as though I have a connection with them in some way, something I can't explain."

"Why don't you ever talk about your family or where you're from. You always avoid the subject, what happened to you, are you hiding from something?" Jack now felt finally compelled to tell her all about his past.

"My parents died when I was young, and my brother died soon after. I was brought up by my elderly grandparents and up to a year ago, I was spiralling out of control." He sighed deeply before taking another sip of wine. "I resented my parents for leaving me like they did, and I rebelled, losing control in the process. Although I was given therapy after they died, I was still having hang ups. I had to leave and find my true self; it was as if I was being possessed by something. If I'd carried on, I don't know where I would be now."

"Jack that's awful," she moved her chair closer cupping his right hand in both of hers. He explained how he had to leave so suddenly without saying where he was going. That he'd been too scared to try and contact his grandparents, following their request for him not to. However, more recently, he kept having this feeling of being called back home. It had been building for a few weeks, but he'd been resisting it.

"You must go back, and you must see your grandparents; they will be worried. Here use my phone, call them now?"

"I can't call them that's the promise I made. I can't return until I've shaken my demons and become the man I'm supposed to be. They said I've a destiny to fulfil but not until I'm ready."

As the atmosphere was broken by a sudden silence, he looked back up to the heavens to watch the stars through his telescope again. "Look see there, the plough."

"What about it?"

"I used to think it was part of Orion's belt, the God that the Egyptians worshipped, but that's over there," pointing. "The pyramids are a perfect replica of the constellation they mirrored when they were first built thousands of years ago. As though they were mapped on the ground from looking down from space. Their burial chambers had small vents leading to the outside, directly in line with the stars above, so the souls of the departed could ascend to the heavens and join Orion himself. It's fascinating, don't you think?"

"Par not really, Jack, no, it's boring and nonsense," pouring herself another glass of wine.

"Is that why you like to look at the stars, do you think you are a spaceman, or do you see your parents and brother there?"

"No, I just see it as sort of chaotic forces fighting each other, like good versus evil but I've no idea why. It's just something that's in me." They sat for a couple more hours listening to the crickets in the darkness and watching the stars in the night sky, until Catherine complained it was getting late and she was cold.

They moved inside to sit in the small lounge area just off the kitchen. "Don't you have any music?"

"No, I've got no music, no devices or phone. I just like things to be quiet and natural."

"Par, you are boring. Just like an old man, what's happened to you. Where's the fun Jack, that we first met?" She took out her phone and spoke into it, asking for some for chill out music to be played and started to dance as the soft tunes started playing.

"Tell me Catherine, you're also a very dark person, never opening up about what you do, are you at college?"

"Non," she said cheekily grinning.

"University?"

"Non." She glided around the table in a flirtier manner.

"Do you live with your parents?"

"Non, I'm only here with my family because I get a free holiday."

"What do you do then?"

"Ha… I work in a club as an exotic dancer," as she continued to dance around.

"I don't believe you, you're far to prim and proper for that."

"Then let me show you," pushing him back into his armchair

and not to move.

She told him to keep his legs apart as she slowly started to remove her tight black dress. She had no bra on, and Jack was already getting excited. She slowly turned, swaying to the music before taking off her thong, which made him swallow hard.

Moving over, she sat on his left knee with her back to him, gently gyrating to the music. Standing again she faced him and pushed his legs further apart. Now kneeling between his legs, she slowly and seductively made her way up his body until they were face to face. As he went to kiss her, she moved to one side, sighing sexily in his ear. Then leaned over whispering for him to go upstairs with her.

She was amazing and kept him going for what seemed like an age. "Now you're a man Jack," she howled in ecstasy. They continued making love all through the night, until eventually exhausted they fell asleep in each other's arms.

Morning came and as he rolled over, Catherine was nowhere to be seen. Walking downstairs he saw a note left on the kitchen table.

Thank you, Jack.
Last night was fantastic and I will never forget you or this holiday. But for me as well as you, it is time to go home. Return to where you belong and make your grandparents proud. Make something of your life—be the man you've now become, find your path and your destiny.

He smiled as he put it back on the table, he now knew what he had to do.

Chapter 6

12 Sept 2016

Arriving at his grandparent's house, he nervously knocked on the front door. Worried how he'd be welcomed after being away for over a year. As it opened, a woman stood staring back at him. She was in her late twenties, but he had no idea who it was. "Can I help you?" she said folding her arms.

"Erm… yes, I'm here to see my grandparents are they in?"

"I'm sorry. Who are you?"

"I'm Jack Johnson, their grandson."

"Oh… right yes… please you'd better come in." The door was quickly shut behind him as he walked into the hallway.

"The place looks different, have they redecorated?"

"Come through and I'll make us some tea. I'm Jackie by the way, take a seat make yourself comfortable." Jack stood in the lounge and didn't recognise anything in the room. He felt a bit awkward, not knowing what he should say or do. He suddenly hear a voice talking and moved closer to the door to hear.

"Yes… it's him I'm telling you… what do I do, get rid of him or tell him?" A short silence followed as someone talked back on her cell phone. "Ok, I'll do that then, I'll give you a call back once we have finished… yes… yes, see you later… love you too." He quickly moved away from the door, intrigued but also slightly nervous. The door pushed open again to the rattle of teacups on a tray. A large white tea pot had his gran's tea cosy on it and there some of favourite bourbon biscuits. The pair sat opposite each other rather awkwardly, waiting for someone to break the silence.

"Tea?"

"Thanks," said Jack. "Erm, where's my grandparents?"

"They're not here anymore I'm afraid," nervously pouring. Making it overflow the cup slightly as her hand shook.

"Are they in a care home or something?"

She looked back with a look of nervousness and concern. "Jack… I really don't know how to do this, so I'm just going say it. I am afraid your grandparents are dead, they both died nearly a year ago. I suppose a short time after you disappeared. Nobody could find you get in touch. The authorities knew you'd gone to France, but then you just seemed to vanish. We were good friends of theirs, me and my husband. We used to help them a lot, fetch groceries, run errands and the like and then when they—" she sighed. "When they died, we were left this house in their will."

"Their solicitor needs to see you as you were mentioned in it as well, there's something for you." Jack sat back shocked, then started to weep. The sudden realisation that he'd also lost his grandparents as well, meant he was now all alone in the world.

"Jack, look at me," she said softly as he lifted his head.

"You had a troubled upbringing and they understood that. You had to go away and find yourself it's okay, they were totally happy about it."

"How did they die?" Jackie held both his hands.

"No-one's a hundred per cent sure what really happened, except they died together in their bed. Holding onto each other, but the only thing is…"

"Yes?"

"Well… it's hard to explain, the coroner put their cause of

death down having heart attacks within seconds of each other, but they looked like they died of fright."

"What?"

"When we came in the next morning to check on them, they… well… they had the look of terror etched on their faces. As if their souls had been suddenly sucked out, as if they'd been scared out of their wits. It was horrific, I'm still having therapy over it now."

Jack still struggling to understand everything, gulped his tea down then sat in silence. "Where are you living now?" asked Jackie.

"Oh… erm just landed back in the country so nowhere yet. I somehow felt I was needed at home again and so here I am, but I guess I'm not really needed anymore?"

Jackie advised it was probably best he didn't stay with them, so he took the details of the solicitor and left to book into a hotel. He'd give the solicitor a call from there in the morning and see what was left for him in the will.

"Good morning, Matthews and Philips how can I help?"

"Oh… Hi yes… I've been given your details to get in touch regarding my grandparents? they passed away a year ago and apparently, I was mentioned in they're will? I'm they're grandson Jack, I've just arrived back in the country."

"Can you tell me their names please and I will see which of the partners to put you through to."

"Yes… its Mr and Mrs Johnson."

"Bear with me please while I just check for you." Jack found the background music extremely annoying, who wants to listen to opera when your important call is on hold. He hated that type of music as well.

"Hello again… Mr Philips was the solicitor who dealt with

73

this, I'm putting you through now."

"Ahhem… morning… Reg Philips how can I help?"

"Hi… My name's Jack Johnson and I'm calling about the death of my grandparents, James, and Silvia. Jackie Osborne, their carer, gave me your details and told me to call?"

"Are yes… Jack… of course… I presume you're getting in touch with regards to your grandparents will?"

"Well yes… apparently I was mentioned in it?"

"Best thing to do, Jack, is pop in really. Now let me see, I'm free this Thursday morning at say nine-thirty? how does that work for you?'

"Sure, no problem."

"Good… good… see you then then, Jack, goodbye."

Jack arrived at the solicitors on cue and waited in reception for his appointment. He looked at the décor and admired the old building. It was still steeped in original features dating back to the 1800s. "Mr Philips will see you now," said the receptionist. "Follow me and I'll take you through," as she opened a door for him. "It's just through there dear, the first door on the right." Jack knocked on the old, varnished door, noticing a brass name plaque at the top, saying Reginald Philips- Partner.

"Come in," came a posh voice.

"Ahh Jack isn't it, please come in… come in… good to meet you finally. You can call me Reg," As they shook hands.

"Sorry for your loss, tragic… very tragic. Take a seat dear boy make yourself comfortable, there's a good chap."

Reg pushed a button on his com, "Philippa, tea for two please… thank you," gesturing for Jack to sit down as he was still standing. He sat surveying the room while Reg made himself comfortable again behind his large desk. The décor again was old with varnished timber panelling, high white skirting boards and green wallpaper on the walls. The ceiling also still had the ornate plaster cornicing and old plaster ceiling roses where the light fittings now sat. The desk was clearly an antique, highly polished with a red inlayed soft leather pad set in the top. With a desk light to match that had a green shade on it.

"How are you then, Jack, we tried everything to find you... you know. People looking everywhere but you had simply vanished. Frightful business with your grandparents... frightful. Anyway, down to business as they say," and walked across the room to remove a painting from the wall. Behind was the predictable wall safe and after spinning the dial around, he opened it.

He took out a shoe box sized carton wrapped in cloth and sat back at his desk, placing it on the edge. Opening the top draw of his desk, he had a rummage around for a while then removed a large envelope. Jack took a sip of tea, sitting inquisitively on the other side of watching.

Holding the will in front of him Reg began. "Now then Jack, as you're aware your grandparents left their house to Mr and Mrs Osborne. They're planning to have children and thought the house would provide them the help and security they need for their future. You know, like a thank you for being their carer's and all that." Waving his hands about almost in a dismissive sort of gesture.

"That's fine," replied Jack. "I probably wouldn't have known what to do with it if they had left it to me anyway."

Reg went on, "I have a gift here for you from your grandparents." Unravelling the cloth that was protecting the box. Inside, were two framed pictures, two letters and another slimmer box. He then read further from the document, "The photographs are to remind you of who you are and where you are from. The framed photograph of your parents and brother were taken while he was receiving specialist treatment for his condition. Your grandparent's wish is for you to treasure this, as it was important to them."

Jack took the frame and stared at the picture, they looked happy despite the circumstances. "Thank you, I'll treasure it," he said.

"The other picture is of you and your grandparents, taken on holiday when you were much younger. Again, they wish you to treasure this as it was important to them, and as they have written here… it will have significant importance for you one day."

Again, Jack said thank you and sat looking at his grandparents faces. "There are two letters as well, with strict instruction not to open them in anyone else's presence." Reg raised an eyebrow as he looked at him, then passed them over. "The slim box here though, this you can open now," handing it over.

It was very old and showing its age. He carefully removed the lid only to be disappointed to find the two gold chains that they used to wear. "Oh," said Reg raising a disappointed eyebrow, expecting something of greater value. Awkwardly saying "Ahem," as he cleared his throat and sat back to continue.

"The sum of £75,000 pounds is left to our grandson Jack Johnson from our estate, on the condition he complies with his parents will."

"There's another will?" queried Jack.

"Oh yes," replied Reg pulling out another sealed document. "We've had this envelope since, oh… way before your parents passed away. They came in to finalise their will when your brother went away for treatment. Leaving strict instruction not to open it until after the death of your grandparents."

He opened the envelope and pulled out a rather small simple penned document, again raising another eyebrow. "Ahem," clearing his throat once more as he began to read. "To our dear youngest child, Jack. We bequeath the sum of £320,000 pounds from our estate. Our remaining estate then going to the institution treating our older son's condition. The strict terms associated with our will are that Jack Johnson, changes his surname with immediate effect to help protect his real identity."

Jack sat back shocked. "What?"

"That is their wish," advised Reg, raising his eyebrows as well in astonishment. "They must have had good reason as to why they wanted this, and we must follow their request if you want the inheritance. I can have the legal documentation prepared ready to sign later today. All you must do now is come up with a new name?"

Jack simply didn't understand but had nothing to lose. He was looking for a fresh start anyway, so agreed to the terms. "Good, pop back around three and we can conclude matters then," As Reg stood directing him towards the door.

Jack left and headed to a wooded park that was opposite. He walked what felt like every inch of it as he pondered on the wills, nothing was making any real sense. What was all the secrecy about, why give him photos and the necklaces, why change his name and what was the significance of it all?

Coming to a pond, he sat on a bench looking at the water and the hungry ducks. "I always find myself drawn to nature when I'm trying to understand or resolve a problem," said a voice from nowhere. Jack turned to see a parson sitting at the other end, breaking off bits of bread to feed the ducks. "You look troubled. You know what they say, a problem shared is a problem halved?"

He passed a chunk of the uncut loaf across, and Jack started feeding the ducks as they came in closer. "The thing is," said Jack. "I had a mixed-up childhood, which led me down a wrong path and it took me a while to realise. I then chose to take a different one and start over. Now, I'm even more confused than ever. Everything I once knew is gone. I should've stayed, I should've looked after them."

"You're not alone, none of us are really," advised the parson. "Only misguided perhaps, but the Lord always forgives us for the sins we conduct." He broke off some bread, throwing it for the ducks who chased across the water to get to it. He smiled as they fought over the floating bits of crust.

"Perhaps you just haven't found your true purpose in life yet, and simply need to continue this new path. Forgetting your past and focusing on the future. Imagine treading a path banked with trees and flowers on both sides. Beautiful yet not tempting enough to divert you from your current course, as you can see an end in the distance. You keep straight but it starts to darken, the trees and shrubbery thickening. Shading out the light until you reach the end where it splits in different directions."

Jack looked at him thinking he was slightly mad but carried on listening anyway.

"You're now stood looking at an old wooden post with direction arrows on it. Go straight on and this is the path you will tread for the rest of your life, darkness and evil being your only companion. Turn left and you go in a different direction an unwritten path, bringing new challenges and opportunities. Turn right and the choice will be slightly different again, perhaps leading you to your true destiny, but to go back is impossible."

"Hmmm, I can relate to that," replied Jack. "The trouble is, perhaps I don't understand this new path and what it requires from me?"

"Sometimes you just need a little divine intervention. To look up to the heavens above perhaps. It's a lovely day, don't you think? not a cloud in the sky." Jack looked up and then in a flash it came to him.

"Sky, of course I'll call myself Sky, with an E on the end though and start a new life. Thanks that was a great help." Turning round to look at the parson, but there was nobody there, just half of an uncut loaf of bread. He smiled to himself not really understanding what had just occurred but felt sure of what to do next and continued to feed the ducks.

He returned to the Solicitors at three as requested and was once more shown into Reggie's office. Reg looked at him grinning in anticipation, waiting to be notified of Jack's new identity.

"I spent a few hours in the park earlier and met a parson of all people. He told me to look to the heavens above for divine intervention and that's when it came to me."

"What did?" asked Reg.

"My new name of course... Skye," he replied. "My new name will be Jack Skye."

"Excellent choice, I have the drafted paperwork here ready. We just have to add the new name in and renounce your old one." As he took his pen out from his pin striped suit jacket.

"Sign here and then here please, and then?" he looked at the documents a little confused for a second, "Oh yes and here... and one here and finally the last one here."

"This document acknowledges that you will no longer be referred to as Jack Johnson. Confirming your new name to be known by hence forth as Jack Skye." With matters concluded, they shook hands and he left with his treasures in a plastic bag and two banker's drafts in his pocket.

Chapter 7

28 Jan 2018

Jack was suddenly awoken by a loud noise; the photograph of himself and his grandparents had fallen to the floor. He'd dosed off with it in his hand while reminiscing. Taking it out of the broken frame, he turned it over. 'Holiday in Cornwall,' was written on it. He was annoyed with himself that he'd dropped it and placing it back on the side table, made a mental note to buy a new frame in the morning.

Taking another sip of wine, he picked up the shoe box and sat back in his chair to have another look inside. He hadn't looked inside for quite a while and still hadn't read the letters. Previously choosing to only take the pictures out. "Alexa, play some chill out music." The room was soon filled with his favourite ambient sounds as he decided to finally read them. Unwrapping the cloth around the shoe box, he lifted the lid off and placed it by his side. With the open box in his lap, he gently put the old slim one to one side and pulled out the letters. Choosing to read the one from his grandparents first and eagerly opened it.

Dearest Jack,

You reading this means we are no longer with you. We hope the money goes a little way to help you find happiness and achieve what you want or need.

We fully understand your need to get away and find yourself and it was something we openly encouraged. We hope that in doing so, you have managed to break free from the demons that were haunting you. Hopefully you are now moving ahead on a path that best suits you. Whatever you do, never forget how much we loved you, including your brother. Even though you never really had a chance to get to know him properly, he was very much a part of your life and tried his best to help while he still could.

The necklaces are a gift, they come as a pair and we hope when you find the right partner, you will both wear them. Just as your grandfather and I once did, there is something special about them. They are very old and were bought during our honeymoon travels back in India. They have a great power, when two lovers wear them, they can share each other's thoughts and feelings. We hope they work for you, Jack you're special, even though, you do not know it yet.

You will face many challenges and in time, a decision will have to be made that will define you as a person for the rest of your life. We hope you can rise to the burden that will be asked of you. Use the photographs as a reminder of your family and happier times as a child growing up and the places, we took you to. Soon you will begin to understand your true purpose and being in life. We hope you face the challenges that lie ahead without trepidation. Embrace what you need to do and never give up, even in the face of adversity. Remember, when all may look lost, there is always another way.

Don't blame yourself for leaving when you did, it is part of the journey you are on. We couldn't be a part of that, it was for you to find your own way on your own. Hopefully the path you are now on has steadied and focused you. Remember, indulging in wrong will only push you down the dark path just like it did before. Learn from the mistakes you made and grow in the light of good not evil.

You will no doubt have lots of questions after reading this, and in time you will look for answers. For now, remember when you look back, that you were loved. You were given time to live your own life before the burden that awaits was placed on your shoulders.

The photos hold the key to unlocking what you feel is missing. When the time comes retrace your steps, follow your instinct and all will become clear.

We will always love you and we will see you again, in another time… it is written in the stars.

Gran and Granddad.

Confused by the riddles, they always talked in; he opened the fragile box and pulled out one of the necklaces. It was clearly ancient, and its links were made of solid gold. Although dull in colour, it seemed to light up as he played with it in his hands. Only for it to fade again when he put it back in the box.

Taking out his parent's letter he started to open the envelope, then stopped and put it back. Resentment entering his mind again, like an old wound reopening. He didn't want to hear what they had to say, they left him years ago, it was too late. Still angry with them, he put everything away, wrapped the box again and put it back on the table next to the photographs. Tomorrow was going to be a busy day and he needed to get some sleep.

He was up before daybreak the next morning and headed out for a 5K run. After breakfast and showering he dressed in one of his smarter casual suits, he had a meeting at eleven with a consortium. They'd previously hired him to find a suitable building for them to develop into a new high-class conference centre. His aim was to try and persuade them to come in as financial partners on the big auction coming up later in the year.

By combining forces, they could hopefully out-bid any others to secure the warehouses and the land. They could then develop or sell on and make a hefty return on top. He would still have to sell his housing portfolio to raise the holding deposit. But with others raising the rest of the capital needed, they could complete on the purchase before the four-week deadline was up.

The only concern in the back of his mind was this new guy on the block, lucifer. What if he did have access to unlimited funds, if he came to the auction, he would lose out on the opportunity to better himself. His mind was turning in circles as he tried to process all the possible variables and outcomes.

Meeting at the warehouses the group walked the outside and down a long alleyway leading to a large central courtyard. Behind were further outbuildings with a few acres of land. He'd done his homework— providing a hard copy presentation of his findings as they walked and talked.

He explained the site was perfectly situated and the warehouses had lots of potential options. They could either develop them into individual flats themselves or simply demolish, making way for new prime residential or commercial sale. It was a good plot with an auction guide price of only £1.8 million.

Either way the sell on potential to larger developers would be attractive. He ran through the spread sheets and figures, explaining how much of a lucrative a deal it could be for them. Even if sold on to a larger organisation or a residential developer. The group were impressed and agreed to discuss it in more detail at their launch party later that evening. Their new conference centre was having its grand opening and Jack had been invited as a special guest. He'd been instrumental in finding the old building for them and securing the deal. They all shook hands and as they slowly dispersed, he could sense their interest and excitement.

Showered and dressed in his favourite black suit, he was ready. Looking smart and dapper, wanting to make a good impression in front of the other guests. The consortium had completed the renovation on time, and he was keen to see the results. He arrived slightly late due to traffic but was welcomed anyway with open arms.

The evening was already in full swing, with both floors full to brim with people. It was an old stately home that he'd managed to find for them. He'd been given the in road it was due to come up for sale at auction and managed to secure the deal privately prior.

He walked around, greeting everybody, showing plenty of interest when introduced to people that he didn't know. "This is Jack Skye, a successful property developer who helped us find this fantastic old building, he's still single you know." Every time he was introduced to any single women.

Jack's reply would always be, "Well, you know how it is, I've just never met the one." Before smiling politely and swiftly moving on. Waiting staff were busy serving cocktails and champagne, while others moved around with trays full of canapes and other treats for the guests. They were dressed smartly in matching uniforms and aprons and a band was playing light Jazz to form a backdrop of soft music.

The mood was high, and the noise of conversation and laughter was a sign that the conference centre would be a success. Jack was happy for them and admired the renovation and new décor as he wandered.

The main grand hall opened to a vaulted space above which looked up to the roof. A large glazed domed lantern then sat on top like a grandiose crown. A staircase rose each side of the grand hall, leading up to a huge four-sided gallery that ran around the first floor. Jack was really impressed with how the renovation works had gone and the quality of the workmanship. Meeting up with the consortium, he expressed how impressed he was as they hugged and kissed. The consortium in return briming with confidence and laughing excitedly.

Before moving on one of them, gently grabbed his upper arm and pulled him to one side. "I heard you were humiliated at an auction, the other day, is everything all right?" Martin was the brains behind the consortium and had become firm friends.

"It's okay, mate, I was outbid on a lot I really wanted, that's all. I think the guy was just out to intimidate me and paid well over the odds for it. It was how he behaved that put me off."

"Listen, Jack, I've heard about this guy, he's bad news. He takes people apart, be careful."

"Thanks for the advice but I think I can take care of myself; do you think the others will come in on the big one with me?"

"I think they will, the figures stack, but they'll further need pacifying as it's a big financial risk."

"Understood," he said as they shook hands before moving on to mingle.

Making his way to the top of the staircase he admired the grandeur and splendour again. The upper balcony area and its glassed dome lantern set in the roof above looked amazing. The building was stunning, oozing glamour and sophistication. The balcony balustrades were also spectacular. He couldn't resist running his hand along the refurbished oak scalloped handrail and observed how the red carpets blended in so well. He could visualise in his own mind how impressive the original building would have once looked. Before falling into rack and ruin when he first got wind it was coming up for auction.

As he stood, a familiar feeling of being watched suddenly came over him. He looked across and on the other staircase, someone was looking back at him. She looked stunning in a tight-fitting black dress as she made her way onto the balcony area. She too ran a hand along the top of the railing as she nodded to acknowledge him, before moving back into the crowd occupying the upper area. Thinking nothing else of it, he took a glass of champagne from one of the waitresses and leaned against the balcony balustrading. Happily watching guests mingling below, occasionally lifting his glass or waving to guests he knew.

His thoughts turned to the consortium again and this character Lucifer. If he could just secure enough funding, he'd should be okay. He felt sure that with the right tact he couldn't be out-bid. Provided he could find a way of putting the other buyers that would be at the auction off. He must have stood thinking for some time, as a waitress suddenly asked if he would like another drink.

A hand gently brushed against his as he placed his empty one onto the tray. Before he could take a fresh one, two full glasses were lifted off with one offered in his direction. "Hi, I'm Leila. You must be, Jack, I've heard a lot about you." She held out her hand ready to shake as Jack stared at her. He was astonished by her beauty she was pure perfection. "Are you all right you look like you've seen a ghost?"

"Sorry just for a second you reminded me of someone I met a few years ago in France. Forgive my poor manners, I'm Jack," taking her hand choosing to kiss it instead of shaking it.

She laughed in return, "Who said romance was dead in the twenty first century?" before taking a sip of champagne. "So, the buzz in here is that you found this place for some friends, who turned it into this fantastic venue, you must be very proud."

"Yes, I am, they've done wonders and I hope they do very

well out of it."

She smiled touching his hand that was resting on the handrail again. "What do you do for a living?" asked Jack. "You seem to know all about me, but I know nothing about you?"

"Everyone knows of you, you're the guy who came from nowhere to make a load of money property developing. You've got the golden touch and your single."

"For me I'm an antiquarian, I study relics and ancient manuscripts." Jack was captivated, not only was she beautiful, but she was also clever too. He wondered if there was also an opportunity to get her to introduce him to any potential funders that she may know.

They stood talking for what seemed like an age, before excusing herself. "Get the drinks in then, the glasses won't refill themselves, you know." Winking as she walked towards the rest rooms.

Martin walked by and quickly leaned in. "Looks like you're off the market finally mate, there'll be women crying all over town tonight. You make a great looking couple."

"Do you know where she comes from Martin, did you invite her, She's stunning."

"No," he said laughing. "It was one of the others, they went to boarding school together and have kept in touch ever since. She doesn't know that many people due to the nature of her work. So, we invited her here tonight to meet new people and now she's met you."

Martin slapped him on his back as he went to walk away. "My work here is done my friend. The rests up you to fuck-up on your own." Quickly moving away as she walked back.

"This is so strange I feel like we've known each other forever," exclaimed Jack. "Are you sure we've never met?"

Leila smiled. "Perhaps it's just fate and you've just met the one, it does happen you know." He laughed back but deep down he couldn't ignore what she'd just said.

"So, Leila, tell me who do you work for and what's involved in the glorious world of antiquarian, I'm intrigued?"

"Well, it's not as glamourous as it sounds really. I work for a small privately owned faction, that, has funding from other small groups. One of the main benefactors pays the lion's share. We get sent all over the world to investigate findings and establish their origins. If they're of historic value, the main benefactor takes the rewards or if they're not interested, they get sold on to the highest biding museums."

"Who's the main beneficiary?" he asked. "Perhaps they'd like to invest with me on some opportunities?"

"We don't know who the actual individual is. Except he's wealthy and well connected, with an insatiable interest in ancient artefacts."

The pair talked for the rest of the evening captivated by each other, ignoring the rest of the party. Jack explained how his life could have gone if he hadn't taken the decision to disappear and re-find himself. How his parents and brother died years ago and how his grandparents had also passed, leaving him on his own. Leila held his hands as he talked, expressing her compassion for what he'd been through growing up.

She explained how she grew up, mostly in the care of others as her parents never really bonded with her. Always too busy with their own lives. Paying all their love and attention to her younger brother until he died in his early thirties. She always felt she was an unwanted inconvenience, growing up sad and lonely. She didn't know where her parents were now, as she'd decided years earlier to make her own way in life.

This was why she'd chosen to do the job she did. It involved long periods of working in isolation, disconnected from normal life. Hence why she didn't know that many people and why her old school friend had invited her. The pair decided to leave the early and headed back to Jack's flat for a nightcap. There was a spark between them, and he wanted to get to know her better.

Opening the front door, he announced his arrival to his Alexa unit. Asking it to play some soft chill out as he turned on the lights and poured two brandies, while Leila inspected the lounge.

"Do you always listen to this music?"

"Well, yes someone introduced me to it when I was in France a few years back, I've listened to it ever since. I suppose it reminds me of the night I was introduced to it."

"Sounds interesting, something you're not telling me?"

"No," he smiled back. "It was just a sort of something and nothing really, but it's stayed with me."

His flat was immaculate and tastefully decorated. "Your flat's very nice but it needs a woman's touch," she explained.

He smiled again as he passed her a brandy, before sitting and taking a sip of his. She continued to inquisitively walk around, putting her glass down every so often. Picking up and feel things, trying to get a better idea of the person she was falling for. "Are these your parents and brother?" picking up a silver framed photo.

"Yeah, it was taken just as my brother fell ill and was starting treatment, we were all happier back then."

"What was his illness?" she asked inquisitively.

"To be honest I'm not really sure, my parents said it was too risky for me to be around him, then sent him away for specialist treatment."

"And this, is this you with your grandparents?" holding up the loose photo.

He sighed, "Yes, they had to bring me up after the accident, they were the closest thing I had to parents."

"Where was it taken, it looks lovely, and you look happy."

"Somewhere in Cornwall I think but I'm not too sure. I don't really remember it."

"Then we must visit sometime, it was a happy place for you." Placing it back on the table then turning to smile with love in her eyes.

Jack then remembered the box. "Oh, I've something that may interest you. Being as you're in the business and all that." Unwrapping the cloth, he lifted the lid off the shoe box.

He took out the old slim box and removed the lid to expose the dull looking gold necklaces. "I was left these in my grandparents will. They said that if I was to ever find the one, you know your true love. Then the lovers would be able to share each other's thoughts and feelings, provided they both wore them." She sat in a chair opposite intrigued, then gasped as he lifted them up, glowing in his hands.

"It can't be surely?"

"Do you know what they are?"

"I think so yes, but… it's… it's just they've been missing for centuries, if they're what I think they are." Gazing at them again, watching them light up as they were handled. "I mean I think I know what it once was?" she replied.

"These… sorry this… I think was the Necklace of Marmonia. In Greek legend it was said that great misfortune would become of its owner. If descended from the queens and princesses of the house of Thebes. It allows any woman wearing it to remain eternally young and beautiful but comes with a curse of course. It was said to have disappeared around 356BC when Phayllus stole it from the temple of Athena. No-one knows what happened to it thereafter."

"Wow," said Jack. "My grandparents apparently acquired them in India, travelling when they were on their honeymoon. The old man, they got them from, told them about special powers that they have." He passed one to her and she studied its beauty, turning it around and around her hand. Making it shine with a bright golden glow.

"Yes, there," she said pointing at the clasp. "See?"
This has been separated from something and a clasp installed, show me the other one," holding out her other hand. Putting the two clasps next to each other, she showed where the necklaces had once been one long chain, then cut to make two smaller necklaces.

She sat down again taking a huge gulp of brandy. "Yes, of course, that would make sense. By cutting the chain and making it into two the powers changed completely. Instead of eternal youth, it now gives the power of telepathy. Enabling the wearers to share their thoughts and feelings." Jack couldn't believe an ancient Greek mythological legend could exist in real life but for Leila, this was why she did the job she did. She went on to explain how myths and legends from the past were very real and how she'd learned this through studying the translations of ancient scrolls and manuscripts.

"Let's try them out then," Jack announced throwing a necklace back over to her. She stood up sheepishly and held it around her neck with the clasps held in each finger.

"Help me put it on," she said nervously. "I don't want to break it." Jack obliged and secured the clasps; Leila then shook her long dark hair back into place around her shoulders.

"Now you," she said gently touching his hand. He put his on and they stared at each other, as the necklaces glowed in deep golden colours before dulling again.

"Well, that didn't work, did it," he laughed awkwardly. "That must mean we're not compatible," before sitting down laughing into his glass before downing the contents. Leila sat and looked across, 'Would you like to make love to me, would you like to see me naked?'
Jack looked up slightly surprised. 'Well yes I would but I didn't think you were that sort of up-front woman?'

'You never asked me?' she replied walking off towards his bedroom. 'I'm just going to freshen up, I'll be back shortly.' leaving him to pour them both another drink.

A few minutes later she appeared, leaning seductively against the side of the door frame to his bedroom with just her black stockings on. 'Well, I'm ready if you are?' briefly looking back as she disappeared into the bedroom. He was up in a flash nearly falling over as he made his way to the bedroom. Bashing into the furniture trying to strip off as he went. She looked perfect as she sat on her knees on the bed.

He knelt next to her and soon they were in full embrace and making passionate love. Finally, exhausted the pair fell back onto the bed laughing. "Did you actually say those things to me in there or was I just dreaming?"

"I never said a word, Jack. I just thought it and you responded."

"I never actually said a word either, it must've been the necklaces, sharing our thoughts and feelings."

They worked, they could feel each other's thoughts and feelings and now they were together as one. In the darkness, the necklaces started to glow once more as the newly formed couple hugged and kissed each passionately.

Chapter 8

Blood of Christ

The big auction was only a few months away and there was plenty of interest in the warehouses on the circuit. Meeting up again with the consortium, Jack unveiled his grand plan to out-bid the competition. He explained he would keep out of sight only coming in at the last minute, to thwart others from starting a bidding war against them.

He wanted the group to place themselves in different places around the room and bid hard from the outset. The idea to push the bids as quickly as possible. The quicker they rose the quicker, the competition would hopefully be put off and fall away. Any remaining serious bidders then having no choice but to either pull out themselves or be forced to bid higher as well.

For larger developers, it would put a squeeze on their overall profit margins. Forcing them to try and recover their losses through a cheaper build process, which would be messy. Whereas for Jack and the consortium, they could work on much smaller percentages as their costs and overheads were much less. He'd worked out the potential sell on value and collectively, they could still push the price high, while turning a good profit on resale.

He'd already put his portfolio up for sale to raise enough capital as a holding deposit. Leaving the consortium to raise the rest to complete and release the deeds. Jack's portfolio was worth £1.3M on paper but he'd settle on around £1.2M if required, to ensure he had the money ready. They all felt they could secure the lots for around £2.0M with a further contingency of £300,000, just in case the bids rose past their targeted plateau.

Concern however was raised by the group that Lucifer could make a show. It had been noted over recent weeks that he'd been buying up property all over. Taking advantage while Jack had been preoccupied with Leila. He assured the group that he wasn't at all worried and was hatching a plan where Lucifer would become unavoidably delayed on the day.

"How will you do that?" asked Martin.

"Distraction of course," announced Jack. "I'll fill you in more on the details once I've come up with the final plan."

The group agreed in principle on the financial arrangements and requirements, acknowledging the risks for all of them in the process. If successful, they would only have four weeks to complete on the sale. Valuable time that was needed to secure the remaining finance or Jack would lose the holding deposit and be left bankrupted. Finally agreeing to move forwards, he invited his lawyer in to confirm the commitment that the group were making together.

"Everyone, this is Reg Philips, he's been my family's solicitor for many years and has been involved with me ever since I first became a property developer."

Reg cleared his throat. "Ahem, Good morning, all. Jack has asked me to produce these documents for you to sign. Just to ensure that we're all aware of the commitment and risks that everyone is undertaking and that the warehouses and land would be quickly sold on. You know dotting the I's and crossing the 'T's and all that."

He smiled at everyone as he finished before raising a disappointed eyebrow due to the lack of response at his attempt at a joke. "Ahem… yes well… I'll leave these with you so that you can review in your own good time of course. Shall we reconvene at another date?" The consortium agreed, and the meeting was concluded as quickly as it began.

Over the course of the next month plenty of interest was shown in Jack's portfolio. He was spoilt for choice with companies falling over themselves to make the purchase. It appeared his reputation, plus the high quality of his portfolio had companies chomping at the bit.

Offers were being made very close to the asking price and after discussions with his trusty lawyer, he agreed to potentially sell. A London based company were the front runners, who managed corporate pension funds. Subject to a meeting and further negotiations, he was happy enough to run with them.

In celebration, he decided to take Leila's advice and go to Cornwall. Revisiting some of the places he'd been to with his grandparents as a child. He needed a welcome break and booked them a weekend stay away. Booking into a Four-star hotel they planned to explore the Lizard peninsular on the Saturday before moving round to see St Michaels Mount on the Sunday, then head back home later the Sunday evening.

She was fascinated by the scenery and during the whole of the first day, his mind was bombarded. Her thoughts and feelings being shared through their necklaces as they explored. Early afternoon they stopped to buy a couple of traditional pasties and sat in the grounds of the lighthouse to take in the views as they ate them. Leila had only recently returned from a brief visit to Hinnom Valley in Jerusalem. Some scrolls dating back thousands of years had been found, only to find when inspected that they were forgeries. She was cross at the amount of time and money wasted and how most of her call outs usually amounted to nothing.

She talked more openly about her work as she ate, remarking about an old Cornish myth. "It's a good job we know what's in these," she remarked humorously, as Jack asked why. "It's said that the devil can never come to Cornwall in fear of being killed and put into their pasties." Jack spat his mouthful out as Leila laughed loudly. Especially when he took a large swig of water from his bottle and choked on it.

He then pounced on her, pretending to force feed her own pasty until it fell apart in their grip. Leaving them rolling around laughing and cuddling, then kissing. Following a lavish meal and a few drinks in the hotel bar. The couple had an early night ready for an early morning start. They needed to be up early to make low tide as they wanted to walk the causeway to St Michaels Mount instead of going over by boat.

On arrival memories started flooding back when he pulled out the old photo of him standing next to his grandparent's. He'd been there more than once but for some reason his mind had blanked it out. The pair made their way across the causeway, holding hands and messing around as lovers do. Blending in with the other sight seers that were also making the visit. Leila was keen to visit the gardens, which Jack had little interest in, but he agreed to look to keep her happy.

Midway through he had a sudden overwhelming feeling. His subconsciousness was telling him to visit the castle, but he strangely felt he already knew it. Leila was busy looking at the plants and how unique they were, due to the mounts micro climate, when she noticed Jack had wandered away. He wanted to go inside to have a good look around and explained the plants were boring him.

She agreed to keep the peace and making their way to the entrance, joined a tour. The tours guide filled his ears with the mounts history, plus more local myths and legends. Moving around inside the castle, she explained about its different rooms before moving them all on to the priory. There she talked of the monks that once roamed there and their simple lives. Yet inside he felt like he'd seen them. Shaking it off as just as dream, they were led to the church.

There he walked down the central aisle, feeling again that he'd been there before. He just couldn't remember when or why or who with. Leila was still with the rest of the group when he heard a noise and a rustling. Turning round to see what it was, he briefly spotted a robed figure before it disappeared.

Wondering what it was, he went over but there was nothing there, apart from the sound of a door closing. Feeling compelled to follow, he moved closer and saw an old door but was then quickly called back by the guide. "This way please sir, let's all stick together please." Feeling slightly embarrassed for leaving the group, Leila welcomed him back, tucking her arm under his as they walked back outside. "What are you like I can't take you anywhere," shaking her head jokingly as they walked back out.

The tour ended and after getting themselves some teas, they sat on a bench taking in the scenery. It had been a perfect weekend but now they faced the long gruelling journey back home. "Thanks Jack it's been a wonderful weekend and it's been lovely here, how's it been for you?"

"Perfect," he replied just as something caught his eye. A robed figure stood by a tree watching. Just before it disappeared, it lowered his hood and Jack got a glimpse of its face. Leila felt his subconscious feelings and asked what was wrong. 'Nothing,' he responded speaking in his mind. 'I just thought I recognised someone but must be mistaken.' The pair headed back across the causeway, laughing, and joking as they tried to beat the tide that was coming in.

For the first hour of the journey home, he was quiet and had zoned out of their subconscious connection. "I can't feel what you are thinking what's up, why can't I feel you?" she said out loud.

"Sorry, I'm not sure how or why, but the connection between us is broken when I think about my family. I've been reminiscing that's all. The visit down here stirred some old memories."

"Is everything all right, darling?" putting a hand on his shoulder.

"Yeah, I've just been remembering my grandparents, that's all."

Opening the central console, he realised he'd left his cell in there all weekend. The signal had been very poor where they were, so he'd turned it off and put it there, forgetting all about it until now.

Switching it on there was a voicemail from Reg. "Hi Jack, its Reg, just to let you know we have a meeting set up for later next week with the company who are keen on your portfolio. Hope you're having had a good weekend and give my love to Leila. Speak when you get back, give me a call dear boy."

Leila wasn't happy he was selling up. She felt his idea of joining forces with a consortium to try and buy the warehouses was stupid and fraught with risk. Jack explained he wanted to do something useful with his life, he owed it to his family. It was a one-off agreement and once the lots were secured, they would be quickly sold on.

He could then focus on undertaking his own developments and building the legacy he'd dreamed of. She had no choice but to be supportive, although deep down she knew he was taking a huge gamble.

It was the day of the initial meeting and Jack was having mixed feelings about selling. He'd toiled so hard to build up his portfolio and wasn't sure anymore if he wanted to sell but concluded it was for the greater good. Leila wanted to go with him for moral support, but he decided he would only take Reg. Just in case things became awkward or difficult. He didn't want her to see him at his worse, when at times he could be quite shrewd and ruthless.

Taking his trusty lawyer with him, the pair headed for an office just off Finsbury Square, after getting to Liverpool Street. "Well, Reg, so this is where all the large corporate developers and construction companies are, perhaps I can sell the warehouses to one of them once I've secured them?"

Reg looked back dismissively. "One step at a time, Jack, one step at a time, don't let greed take over."

They located the small office block situated in the corner of a square and signed in at the plush reception. They made their way to the top floor by lift, where they were met by a very helpful receptionist. "Take a seat Gentlemen, I'll notify your arrival, you shouldn't be kept waiting for too long, they're just finishing off an internal meeting." The pair looked at each other with Reg raising an eyebrow as they sat down to wait.

"Is this sort of thing normal, Reg, keeping us waiting like this?"

"Yes, quite normal, don't worry... just relax... I've got your back. There's nothing to worry about, they're just trying to take the power hand and make you feel vulnerable."

After ten minutes Jack had counted all the ceiling tiles in the grid above him. How many power points there were, how many carpet tiles were on the floor and had scrutinised the colour scheme. Finally, the receptionist reappeared asking them to follow her. She took them to a large glass fronted office that had the blinds down. Knocking on the door a voice came from inside, "Enter," and she quickly went in, closing the door behind her. Reg placed a hand on Jack's shoulder. "Here we go then, just keep it calm it will all be good."

"Thanks, Reg, I still get a little nervous meeting people I don't know for the first time, especially when there's so much money at stake."

The door re-opened and the receptionist appeared again, smiling at them. "You may go in now gentlemen," smiling again as she closed the door behind them once they entered. Jack quickly scanned the surroundings, noticing its clean white crisp finish. He could also what looked like collector's items, placed on individual display tables. An old Chinese vase, a cluster of fossilised eggs, a crown and what looked like an old Roman soldier's helmet along with some other weird items.

In front of them a large glass table was fully set up with the latest IT equipment and piles of stacked paperwork. An individual was sat in a black leather chair but had its back to them. In the windows reflection they could see a man sitting with his hands together, touching his lips with his outstretched fingertips, almost in a state of contemplation.

"Sit down, gentlemen—I'll be with you in a minute," came a soft calm voice.

"Nice collection," said Jack trying to hide his nerves.

"Thanks, I've a bit of a fascination when it comes to history and civilisation. Collecting its memorabilia is one of my hobbies. Please there's no need to stand on ceremony, sit down gentlemen, make yourselves comfortable."

Jack feeling slightly awkward decided to break the strange awkwardness. "We haven't been formally introduced, I'm Jack Skye and this is my lawyer, Reg Philips."

Just as he was finishing the chair spun round. "Hi Jack, nice to see you again." A face he recognised beamed a sarcastic smile, taking him completely off-guard.

"Lucifer," he shouted, "Fucking hell, we're out of here, Reg, let's go." Pushing his seat back so hard that it fell over as he stood up. Lucifer held both his hands up gesturing for calm. "Now... now... Jack, come on, please. Sit down let's not make a scene. I think we got off on the wrong footing before, let me explain myself."

Reg nodded to Jack, giving him a look if to say it was okay, here him out. Lucifer then sat forwards leaning on his elbows and touching his fingertips together again. Slowly moving them backwards and forwards, touching his top lip. Watching as Jack regained his composure before tilting his head slightly, looking into his eyes gauging his mood.

Jack was now uncomfortable and nervous, trying hard to hold his nerve. "What is it with me, what's the fascination. How did you know my old identity when we first met?"

"Look Jack, people change their identities all the time it doesn't matter. I just like to do my research when I am interested in someone, I need to know about them. I'm a businessman after all and what else I can say, I'm interested in you." Staring into Jack's eyes again.

"I watch people and sometimes feel the need to antagonise them. You know to get a feel of what makes them tick." Tilting his head again—inquisitively drilling into Jack's face further with his eyes.

"I didn't mean to come across so arrogant and obnoxious but

101

unfortunately on the day we met, I'd been on the go for over twenty-four hours. Trying to finalise a deal with someone giving me the run around. The cocaine kept me awake but made me a bit crazy in the process. I apologise for my manner it was unprofessional of me."

He rang through on his intercom and arranged for refreshments, then changed the subject to the ornaments he had on display.

"So, you like my collection. I've spent many years acquiring them, let me tell you about them while we wait. The vase over there is from the Ming dynasty, dating back to 1567 and the Jiajing period; the fossilised eggs over there are sixty-five-million years old and came from Ravioli, Gujarat in India. Where it's thought to be the biggest dinosaur nesting nursey ever found, at twenty-square metres in size."

He then moved to the crown. "This is a Russian orthodox crown that belonged to the Romanov Zsar family. Oh, and this item here is one of my favourites and extremely rare. I was lucky to secure it," as he picked it up to admire it.

"This helmet is said to have belonged to one of the Roman soldiers from Christ's crucifixion. He was killed for being a secret follower of Christ, having been caught visiting the tomb where his body was laid out. The tomb and helmet were found a few years ago but kept secret from the public domain for obvious reasons."

"Are you saying that Christ was real?" questioned Jack.

"If you believe it's real then its real." As he put the helmet back on its stand.

"Ah and this," as he picked it up. "This skull is said to be from a dead devil hunter, an occult sort of following. The only people apparently capable of killing the devil." Turning and smiling, before lifting it up to look at it inquisitively. "Of course, if you believe in that sort of thing. Nice bone structure, don't you think? such a waste," as he ran a finger down its cheek. Looking slightly saddened and tearful, as if almost in mourning for it.

Finally, he pointed to his desk where a tatty old looking whip lay. It was completely weird, shaped in the form of a wrist and fist bound in old leather.

"This is my absolute favourite," he said, picking it up admiring it. "The fist of God, this ancient object has the power to throw lightning strands from its knuckles as you crack it. It's supposed to be so terrifying, that if the strands hit and envelop you, they'll rip the soul clean from your body." He looked almost excited at its prospect.

"Does it work?" enquired Jack, almost disbelieving his words. Lucifer gave it a flick as though using it like a real whip, but nothing happened.

"I suppose not," smiling to himself as he put it back down on his desk.

The office door opened, and a trolley, full of delights were pushed in. "Ah... refreshments," clapping his hands together as he sat down again. "Shall I be mother?" Jack had an Earl Grey and Reg had his usual black coffee. While Lucifer however, poured himself a whiskey over ice and sat back in his chair. Rolling the glass around, so the ice made a clunking sound.

"Now then, Jack, there are two reasons why I've asked you here today. Firstly, a question about the sale of your property portfolio?" leaning forward.

"Why would you suddenly be selling, it's worth a great amount of money and from the information I've gathered, you've put your whole life into this building it up?"

Jack now feeling his confidence returning also leaned

forwards.

"It's time to sell up and move into a different league, you know, take a few risks. I've no family so why not?" Shrugging his shoulders.

"I can relate to that, I'm not family man either. I tried it oh many…. many…. years ago, now. Before being pulled in a different direction to where I am today. I like the freedom of coming and going as I please, you see. I'll tell you what, I like the cut of you, Jack, I'm therefore happy to pay you the full £1.3 million on the proviso that you still manage and maintain them for me?"

He stared at him waiting to see his response, but Jack stayed quiet. Forcing Lucifer to screw his face up slightly in disappointment. Reg now came to the throes, advising he would need to take this offer away and review with his client as it was such an unusual request. Lucifer flicked his hand acknowledging the request but almost dismissing it at the same time.

"The second reason why I've asked you here is to try and employ your services. Come and work for me here," spreading his arms wide open looking upwards. "Work within an organisation that lives hard, parties hard and…"

"Fucks hard by any chance?" Jack replied sarcastically as he piped in. Lucifer intrigued by his remark tilted his head slightly and grinned.

"Well, if you put it like that, yes if that's what you want?"

"No thanks, I trod that path a long time ago and I'm not going there again." Jack once again pushed his seat back to make a move to leave. "Thanks for your time and offer but I think we're all done here now."

Again, Lucifer held his hands gesturing for calm. "Okay, I'm sorry if I offended but I had to ask. How about I employ you on a freelance basis instead then? Leaning forwards with his hands together again. "To look at some prime auction properties and potential land acquisitions that I've got an eye?" Jack still stayed quiet and stony faced.

"You see, Jack, my work takes me all over the place, which then takes up a lot of my time. as you can imagine. Let me tell you, it takes plenty of soul searching at times, travelling from one place to another, if you get my drift," looking at him again to gauge any signs of reaction. "I need someone I can trust, who can attend things on my behalf. Secure some lots that are of extreme importance to me."

"You're a competitor of mine, why should I help you?" Jack replied.

"Well let me put it to you like this, I could make you very rich, very quickly, but refuse my offer. Well, I'd be left with no choice but to make life difficult. Buy everything you try and go for moving forwards perhaps. You see money's no object." He said as he stood and started to walk around his office again. "I could put you out of business and ruin you, if I wanted. But I really don't want too so how about it?"

Jack was shocked and continued to just sit in silence. Reg looked at him concerned then turned to Lucifer who was now staring back at him. Tilting his head slowly from side-to-side as he drilled into his eyes. Reg began feeling an uneasy coldness running through him. As though a vision of his future had just been planted in his mind while he was being stared at.

Lucifer then turned back to Jack. "The first lots that I would want you to bid on are some parcels of land. Not for development but to be left untouched. I want these protected and will pay handsomely to secure them."

Jack was really confused. "Why would you buy parcels of

land that have no financial benefit to you?"

"Their importance is of far greater importance to me than the money they'd generate. Let's just say it's a much longer-term investment, to help preserve and secure my future."

"The second lots that I wish you to bid on are some large old warehouses with land to the back of them. I'm sure you know the ones in question." Again, staring at him before turning away and sitting back at his desk. "There's a large auction coming up soon, that they'll be in. I would want you to secure these for me."

Jack felt an icy shiver run through him, was Lucifer on to him, had his own grand plan being blown wide open?

"There's no immediate rush of course... but... I will need an answer by the end of the week," as he looked at his watch. In the meantime, if you'll excuse me please gentlemen. I have a rather pressing engagement with something that requires my own personal intervention."

He got up from behind his desk, making his way to another door before briefly turning. "The individual I'm going to see is quite literately going to die when he sees me. I trust you can see yourselves out." giving the pair a wide smile. He then slicked his black hair back with his bony fingers, opened the door and disappeared inside.

Jack jumped up and ran over knocking on it loudly, he had questions to ask - he wanted more answers but there was no response. He turned the handle and peered inside, but it was a box room, barely big enough for two and completely bare. Lucifer was nowhere to be seen and there were no other doors in or out.

"Did you find him?" questioned Reg as he returned.

"No, he's nowhere to be seen and I can't find how he got out, it must be a trick room of some kind."

"That's not all that's missing," said Reg, pointing to where the whip had sat.

"Come on Reg let's get out of here, I've had enough of his weirdness and theatrics."

The pair were shown back to the lifts and signed out at the ground floor reception, before heading back to Liverpool Street. Neither said a word as they walked, their brains fried, frantically processing the events of the meeting. At the station, Jack picked up a take-away tea and cinnamon loop, while Reg had settled for his usual black coffee. Taking the odd sip, before burying his head behind his newspaper on the train.

The train slowly headed off, gently rocking from side to side as it made its way out of the city, then sped up to head back towards the countryside. Thumbing the top of his cup, Jack was in deep thought. Taking the odd bite of his pastry and sip of tea as he stared out of the window. Every so often Reg looking over his paper to take a slurp of coffee, then disappearing back behind it again.

With Jack in a world of his own, Reg eventually broached the elephant in the room. "Ahem," clearing his throat as he shook the paper. "Four down... five letters... another name for Satan?"

"Sorry, Reg, what? my name has four letters in it not five?"

"No... no... no... the clue in the crossword, another name for Satan, five letters!"

"Oh, for god's sake, Reg, it's the devil."

"Exactly and that's who you are dealing with here!"

Jack just laughed back at him. "What a load of bloody rubbish, the guy's an eccentric with some underlined issues going on that's all. I almost feel a bit sorry for him, trapped in that mind."

"I hope you know what you're getting yourself into. I don't

trust him one iota. I recommend you walk away before he takes full control."

Jack however wasn't listening, his eyes transfixed and wide-open. As though he had just had an epiphany as he leaned forward slapping Reg on his shoulder.

"Finally, I have a plan that can work. I get the cash I need to secure the deposit by selling to him and then pretend to work for him. The consortium can bid on my behalf while I bid for him. Only I'll never bid high enough, it's a win, win scenario."

"Hmm?" grumbled Reg, raising a disapproving eyebrow. "There are a few issues with that logic, you're getting above yourself," shaking his paper again as he hid behind it. Jack sat staring at him as a few seconds later, he dropped it again to continue.

"The deal with the consortium still hasn't been completed and the sale of your portfolio is yet to be finalised. If you do work freelance for him, he has unlimited access to money. So you'll always be able to bid higher, how do you suggest you resolve that one then smart arse?" Raising both eyebrows in a discourteous manner.

"Well, my old friend, it's quite simple really. The consortium will sign the documents you've produced, once they learn I have control of Lucifer, that's a given." Turning again to look out of the window, briefly watching the countryside pass by before continuing. "Speak to his people, get them to incorporate some amendments to the terms and conditions of the contract before I'm prepared to sign on the dotted line."

"These terms being?" quizzed Reg, folding his arms.

"I'll agree to manage my old portfolio as requested but only for a further year, with a management figure yet to be agreed. The payment for the overall sale to be paid by BACs into my account by close of business on the day of signing." He stopped for a few more seconds thinking further before carrying on again.

"I'll also act on his behalf at any auctions or land sales that he requests me to, caveated. I'll only ever bid up to a maximum of £2Million and I'll also take a ten per cent fee for any bids won on that basis."

Reg stared back at him shaking his head. "I think you've no idea who you're dealing with here. You're doing a deal with the devil, and you don't realise it. I hope you don't end up selling your soul in the process."

Reg opened his newspaper again, giving it, another shake before disappearing behind it for the rest of the journey. Jack was then left to his own thoughts as he stared out of the window again. The only breaks in silence being made by the occasional "Ahem," as Reg cleared his throat or the odd grumble as he muttered to himself every so often. "Stupid… no idea… no idea at all."

Back at his flat he shared his plan with Leila, who also advised he must be mad. She pleaded with him not to do the deal, "Be happy with what you've got, Jack, you don't need to do this?" but she couldn't get him to see sense. He'd changed, suddenly he was vain and greedy and she didn't like it.

"Look what he's already turning you into, please just do what Reg said and walk away. You know nothing about this guy he sounds really risky."

"Leila its fine," putting his hands on her shoulders. "This opportunity gives me the chance to build a legacy in memory of my family."

"Jack, please, I love you, don't do this. I can't stand by you on this, it's too risky please just walk away, I beg you." Instead, he pushed her away, his voice firm and cold.

"No… I'm not backing down just because you two are scared. The guy's got a few loose screws that's all and I'll take him down."

She couldn't bear to see him like this; it was a side she'd not seen before, and she didn't like it. Deeply upset she knew she had to get out and left, going back to her own apartment for some space.

Although Reg wasn't happy, he did as asked and by the Wednesday afternoon, a deal in principle was in place. Provided of course Lucifer could agree to Jack's amended terms. A meeting was therefore set up for the Friday lunchtime at his offices in London.

On the day, Reg could tell Jack was anxious. Instead of talking, he spent the whole train journey silent. His left knee nervously bounced up and down as he stared out of the window, chewing on his fingertips. The day before hadn't gone at all well with the consortium.

They were showing a clear nervousness about the deal and wanted more time to think things over. The risks involved were very high and they needed more time to consider all their options before committing to sign up or not. Either way there was no going back now for Jack. He had no choice but to front it out, hoping that everything would then fall into place.

The pair received a warm welcome at the offices and were shown to a plush looking meeting room full of refreshments. Lucifer was running late so his team were given the task to entertain while they waited. They were most accommodating and jovial, which helped put Jack's nerves at rest. He tucked into the Italian pastries and happily talked about his career to date. His home life and other subjects raised, almost as though the team knew every single detail and how to woo him.

Reg though noticed something odd about Jack's behaviour, and after interrupting the conversation with an "Ahem", and a "Please forgive the interruption, may I have a quick word with my client outside please." Grabbed him by the arm and walking him to the toilets.

"What's up with you. One minute you're like a frightened little schoolboy and the next acting with more confidence than I've ever seen you with, what's going on?"

Jack sniffed saying he was fine as he threw a small wrapper into the bin.

"Oh no, Jack, what the hell are you playing at?"

"It's all good I needed a little extra courage, so I took a wrap of coke to settle my nerves... don't worry yourself," slapping him on his back. Reg had never sworn at Jack before, but he couldn't hold back any longer.

"You selfish, greedy little cunt! You're going to jeopardise everything you stupid fucking little shit." Walking out slamming the door as he went. Jack quickly caught him up, saying he was sorry, and the pair walked back into the meeting room.

Lucifer had also finally arrived, "Sorry for the lateness everyone, I had a very late night." Winking at one of his personal assistants, who immediately turned red with embarrassment. Knowing their dirty little one-night stand was now out in the open.

"Well, welcome everyone and thank you for keeping our guests here entertained in my absence," he said clapping his hands together. "Shall we take some refreshments before getting down to business?" Looking at each of his team in turn as he took their orders, then moved round Reg and Jack's side of the table. "Tea, coffee, Reg?... oh no... you're just black coffee aren't you," His team smiled as though a private joke had just been

111

shared. Reg raised an eyebrow as some further sniggers were heard. "Ahheemm" and with that the table erupted in laughter as Lucifer smiled and moved on to Jack.

"And… finally to the main man himself… tea… coffee or some Coke perhaps, Jack?"

"Just a Diet Coke, thanks." Again, sniggers were heard from around the table.

"Really… haven't you had enough already this morning or was it just diet coke in your breakfast wrap?" as he stared at him, more sniggers came from the table. "Okay, shall we get down to business then." Sitting down and opening his copy of the contract for review. "So… I see here you've added some of your own terms and conditions, hey Jack?"

"Yep," he replied, capping his hands together on the table.

"Hmm," he said as he read. "Well, who's a greedy boy then?" looking up and staring at him intently.

Reg quickly interjected. "As Jack's lawyer, the terms added are not considered unreasonable and are in fact a fair inclusion to the proposal you first offered."

"Yes… yes… I get all that," said Lucifer, waving his hand dismissively. "But what is your fee for the years management of the existing houses then?"

Before Reg could respond, Jack rudely butted in. "I want £350K to manage my old stock once sold to you."

"Oh… someone's finally found their tongue haven't they!" Lucifer responded as he put his head to one side staring at him.

"The thing is with that sort of demand I now have to rethink the overall value of the sale?"

"There's nothing wrong with my property portfolio it's well maintained and well managed, hence the value it was given. You'll have no problems; I can stake my reputation on it… take it or leave it!"

Reg cut across, "No, Jack, don't say things like that, not to this person," but it was already too late.

"Pride before a fall, eh. You have balls, Jack, I like that, what about staking your soul?" Staring hard, almost drilling into his face with his eyes. Jack suddenly felt unnerved and concerned. "Only joking, I just wanted to see your reaction. Tell you what, Jack, I'll take you up on that offer," and wrote £350,000 in the blank spaces of both documents and initialled them.

Lucifer's lawyer continued, running through the finer contract clauses of the sale, honing-in on one important clause.

"The contracted agreement may be terminated by either party, at any time, now or in the future. At any point of the said agreement being breached by either party as further caveated. This being any wrongdoing undertaken or implemented by either party, will be fully compensated in full by the offender. To the offended, within a timescale that is to be agreed by the said offended party. That being that the other party has/ was/ being unlawfully wronged by the other."

Jack looked at Reg and whispered, "What the hell does that all mean?"

"It's legal jargon," whispering back. "It just means there's a protection clause for both parties to ensure the agreement is honoured... do you wish them to continue, or do you want to withdraw?"

"You're my lawyer, Reg... shall I?"

Reg stood up and addressed the table. "Can we call a quick comfort break please, I would like a few minutes with my client again in private, if you don't mind". Lucifer agreed to a ten-minute break, advising he'd arrange for more refreshments.

As the pair shuffled and squeezed behind people and chairs,

113

Lucifer made a remark, "What's it to be Reg... Black Coffee again?" Reg nodded. "And for you, Jack, tea or would you perhaps like some more Coke?" Jack was suddenly paranoid, did he mean the drink or more cocaine to sniff up his nose. Reg opened the meeting room door and gently gave him a push to ensure he quickly left.

In the toilets Jack frantically washed his face with cold water, trying to make him refocus. "I asked for a protection clause to be installed into the contract, so if Lucifer made a play to ruin you, you were protected. However, the same applies for him as well," said Reg as he stood at the urinal.

"It's your choice whether you wish to continue or not but bear in mind the plan you're trying to action behind closed doors. If it's proven you were plotting against him for your own personal gain, then you could become liable for any loss suffered. I cannot tell you how to proceed but I would think very carefully before you go back in there."

Reg washed his hands as he looked in the mirror, staring hard at Jack in the reflection.

"He's spooked you, hasn't he?" asked Jack. "That day when we met him in his office. He looked at you strangely and you haven't been the same since, what's going on?'

"It's nothing, he got into my psyche that's all, which unnerved me a bit. I could somehow see my future and I didn't like what I saw."

Jack put his hands-on Reg's shoulders, "What did you see Reg... tell me... you're my closest friend."

"My death Jack... I saw my death," shrugging Jack's hands off his shoulders and walked out of the toilets.

Jack started to feel slightly uneasy as he tried to laugh off the comment to himself, heading back to the meeting room. Inside he could see the others patiently waiting for his return, as Lucifer moved both copies of the contract in front of him. A small tray was laid out with an ink well and a fountain pen next on it. Taking a deep breath, he made his way back in, edging his way along behind the chairs again.

"Ah, Jack, welcome back… we were beginning to think you'd left us; shall we proceed?" Reg looked at him secretly hoping he'd decline the offer, but Jack had other ideas.

"Let's get on with it shall we," as he took his seat again. Reg swallowed hard, as he shook his head in disbelief. He couldn't share with him what he'd seen in his vision as it was too horrific. A laptop was passed across to Lucifer by one of his financial team and he spun it around. Showing all parties as witnesses that the sum of £1.3M was ready for BAC's transfer as soon as the button to send was pushed.

Taking the pen off the tray he undid the lid and inserted the nib into the ink well. Squeezing the membrane above the stylus, it sucked a small amount of the liquid ink into the pen's vial. Lucifer's lawyer then advised him to sign and date where the crosses were, then initial each page at the bottom and date accordingly. Both copies were duly signed, then passed across for Jack to sign.

He reached into his jacket, pulling out his favourite pen when Lucifer stopped him, placing a hand over the document. "Please, Jack, use this one, I insist. I use it to close out all my legal and business agreements," pushing the tray across. Jack looked at the documents in front of him and noticed the signature and the printed name of Lucifer Diablo MD, with his next to it.

Picking the pen up he dipped it in the ink well, squeezing the vial to draw some more of the liquid up. "Blimey this inks very weird, where does it come from?"

Lucifer sat with his elbows on the table and his hands together in front of his face. "This inks far better than anything else, even better than the ink used for registering births and deaths it lasts forever and never fades."

Jack signed the first copy, finishing off by initialling and dating, before moving to the second. Stopping briefly to recharge the pen and pull the second document closer. Lucifer sat quietly watching before turning to Reg. Staring at him hard as he tilted his head slightly, while Jack signed the other copy.

"I purchased the ink you're using from an old man in India many… many years ago. He called himself the prophet if I remember. I paid a king's ransom for it; it's believed to be the blood of Christ. The vile is said to be the only one in existence, suspended below his cross to catch the droplets of blood as they ran down his body, of course, if you believe in that sort of thing," he jested. The room fell silent as Jack dropped the pen, wiping his hand up and down his trouser leg as if he had blood on it.

With the signatures complete, Lucifer pushed the send button on his laptop and the funds were transferred. "Congratulations, Jack Skye, you're now a wealthy man, what was once yours is now mine, closing the laptop. "As we're one big happy family now, why don't we all go out for a late lunch to celebrate… my treat." Reg shook his head slightly at Jack to say no, but Jack was on a power trip, drunk with greed and gluttony.

"Sure… why not I am a little hungry."

Lucifer smiled, "That's the nibbles, Jack, what you need is some more Coke to take that edge of again," giving him a wink. Jack was embarrassed and tried to dismiss it by denying any knowledge of what he was talking about, but Lucifer responded jokingly, "It's all right, Jack, you're amongst friends here." As he spread his arms out in an arc, acknowledging everyone around table. "No one cares, we all do it here," and the table erupted in laughter.

He then rang through on his comms, giving orders for the receptionist to book a table for fifteen at his favourite restaurant for around two-thirty p.m. Minutes later and the call came back with confirmation of the booking at the Dorchester, with rooms also booked. Just in case guests wished to stay on and go on to his club in the evening.

Chapter 9

Manipulation

The wine flowed as the team of waiters tended to everyone's needs. Despite Jack and Reg drinking plenty of water during the meal. They were starting to get drunk by late afternoon, but Lucifer wasn't done yet. Toasts followed dessert as he asked for glasses to be raised for Jack. He wasn't only a wealthy guy but was also going to help the company on a freelance basis.

Reg leaned over saying he was too drunk to drive when they got back home, so felt that perhaps they should stay the night as rooms were already booked. Jack wasn't so keen though, he wanted to get back to make sure Leila was okay. He hadn't felt her thoughts since she walked out after their argument. His necklace also hadn't glowed to show that they were still connected. He just wanted to see her and patch things up.

Lucifer overhearing the conversation, offered to take them with some others to a club he owned. There they could continue the party to which Reg immediately agreed. Jack had been trying Leila's phone on and off all day, but it was going straight to voicemail. He was annoyed about it so agreeing to stay over wasn't so much of an issue, he felt it was a bit of pay back. So, he texted her to say they were staying in London for the night. Adding he would catch up with her as soon as he got back.

The club was in an old, converted warehouse spread over two floors. Small bars and seating areas were strewn around the perimeter of the ground floor, giving plenty of space for people to mingle. This then led into another larger main bar area with plenty of tables and lounging sofas. Including a dance area and what looked like a mock-up of a stage. Wide screens played music videos and people were taking it in turns to sing on the stage. Trying to attempt their best renditions of their favourite artists.

The main club itself was set on the first floor, spread across the whole area with a high roof space. The main theme bar below erupted as Lucifer appeared. Leading the entourage to the VIP area they sat, taking up all the spare lounging sofas. Waitresses dressed in lycra shorts, tight fitting tops and long socks, busily zoomed around on roller skates. Delivering drinks to waiting tables, whilst other party goers opted to huddle in rows two or three deep. Trying to get cheaper drinks direct from the main bar instead of paying for premium table service.

A party goer was singing to her favourite song on the stage but was badly out of tune. The crowds jeering as she took the walk of shame back down off the stage. Lucifer then jumped up quickly announcing it was his turn and made his way to the stage. The crowd shuffled to the front as he picked the mic up off the floor, getting a little feedback through the speakers in the process.

He tapped it a couple of times before shouting into it, "Can you hear me!" Holding his arms up high as the crowd screamed back at him. A track began to play, and Reg knew it straightaway, folding his arms and raising his eyebrows. 'It had to be didn't it… Rolling Stones… Sympathy for the fucking Devil." Jack looked at him both in surprise and astonishment. Not only did his friend know the song, but he'd also sworn for the second time in as many days.

The crowd went mad as he finished, standing with his arms

out as though in a crucifix position with head bowed low. As the roar continued, he dropped the mic onto the stage floor, screaming feedback through the speakers as it bounced. The crowd then roaring again like they were paying homage to a rock god.

Re-joining the group, he asked if anyone else fancied a turn but there were no takers. Turning to Jack and Reg, he shouted above the noise of the music. "It's all about showmanship, boy's, you see them now, they can't get enough of it." As he pointed around the room. "The more they want, the more they drink, lining the tills in the process. Let's move on up to the club upstairs, it's got a bit of everything for everyone you'll love it." With that the group were swiftly gathered up and shown the way to the first floor.

The club was dark with blue mood lighting around the perimeter, helping to cast shadows for extra effect. Women danced on podiums and in large cages, hung from the vaulted roof above. Every so often plumes of smoke and fire exploded from different areas, giving a sense of mystery and alienism. Difficult choreographed dances were being performed, while contortionists rotated on small circular platforms and half naked women danced on poles.

A further area was set well back, almost hidden from view, which was far seedier. Lap dancers and prostitutes prowled, looking for single men or offers on couples looking for swingers. Taking them away to special booths where you could see through back lit curtains. The silhouettes of their bodies cavorting clearly on view, all designed to make you let go of your inhibitions.

Reg had clearly let go of his as he was seen making his way over to the lap dancing section. He was then led away by a very beautiful looking dancer for his own personal dance session. Jack could see the silhouette in the booth as she got down to business and was surprised, he still had it in him.

Now alone Lucifer sat down next to Jack and threw some wraps, pills, and LSD onto the table.

"You're quiet, the Coke must be wearing off. Have some more or even try a pill?" rubbing his hands. "Or how about a trip, you used to love them in Amsterdam?" Looking for a reaction.

"How do you know what I used to get up to in Amsterdam?"

"I told you, Jack, I like to know everything about a person, you could almost say I was even there once with you."

He swung round and stared hard at Lucifer, who in turn tilted his head grinning. Finally, he'd got to him and enjoyed seeing such a reaction. Drunk and losing control, he couldn't stop himself reaching down to pick up the drugs. He looked at the Ecstasy and swallowed the pill, then placed the trip under his tongue. It tingled slightly as the LSD started to slowly release and with a quick slurp of champagne, washed everything down. Lucifer's eyes lit up with excitement and anticipation, now it was just the wait to start coming up.

The music got deeper and slightly darker as the beat started to rush through his body. Before he knew it, he was on the dancefloor, remembering the feelings he used to have when he was younger. The LSD was starting to kick in as the music slowed, getting deeper and dirtier. He could see shapes and shadows moving around the walls cast by the back lighting. Strange looking creatures like demons, dancing and swaying with their eyes wide open, red and beast like. An old familiar look now bared down on the women as they danced. Faces morphing from beauty then to beast, hands moving and caressing their bodies from under their skin.

Suddenly he needed somewhere to calm himself down and

saw a room with a sign above saying, 'chill out zone'. He headed straight in and finding a large sofa to sit on, collapsed into it. It was squashy and comfy as he sunk into it. Making his body rush as it moulded itself around him, as the hallucinations began. The LSD rushing through his body as he started to open his mind' just as he did when he used to see visions.

A full height mirror opposite caught his eye and the more he tried to ignore it, the more it tempted. Until he was finally transfixed, staring at his own reflection. The image wobbled and shimmered, then disappeared to reveal a place he'd seen many times before. An old room painted white, a bed, a chair, a desk, and a candle for light. A person was sat with their back to him at the desk. It was the same hallucination of his dead brother again, only this time he was older, and he could also reach in and feel the old painted stone walls. The smell of the dampness came through as well as the candle flickered, and shadows danced on the walls.

A chill suddenly came over him as he felt something push him aside. "Peak a boo," came a voice next to him, the figure at the desk then spun round in surprise. "Lucifer… how did you… Jack?" Lucifer stared with a huge wide evil grin and Jack recognised it straight away. He'd seen it when he was in the bar in Amsterdam years ago.

"I can get to you whenever I want now, John." Climbing through to squat on the edge of the opening formed by the mirror. "They can't hide you from me forever."

"No!" shouted John, throwing a large vial of water.

The vision disappeared at once and suddenly Jack was staring at his own reflection again but soaking wet. Lucifer appeared next to him also dripping wet. Slicking his hair back into place with his bony fingers. "Well, that was all kind of seriously fucked up don't you think? … Woh… what a rush!"

Jack didn't know what was going on, was that real or was it another one of Lucifer's crazy mind tricks. Letting the drugs do their bit knowing he was hallucinating. Either way he needed to get out some fresh air, but as he headed along the edge of the dance floor, the music changed again. He once again felt the uncontrollable need to dance and was dragged back into the middle by a couple of beautiful women.

He moved round and round, staring at the different faces in the club. Reg could be seen in the background having the time of his life but for Jack it felt like pure hell. The girls grabbed his hands and started to move in a tight circle. The three of them moving faster and faster until everything became a blur as they let go of him. He felt his mind spinning, dizzily out of control and could feel himself falling, until he landed with a heavy thud on the floor.

It was now morning, and he was on the bedroom floor of the hotel room, he'd just fallen out of bed. His head pounded as he propped himself against the side of the bed, trying to get his bearings. He noticed a dress laid over a chair and the sound of someone having a shower. He sat quietly as the shower stopped and a pair of legs walked back into the room. He managed to stand to see who was there, hoping it was Leila.

"Hi sleepy head, did you fall out of bed? I'm surprised you can even stand up this morning, you were an animal last night." It was the wife of a swinging couple that he'd seen reg with.

"Where's your fella?"

"Oh… don't worry, he didn't come back with us. He went off with an older guy and another beauty for a threesome."

"What Reg did?"

"Yes, that was his name, very posh and well spoken."

"Blimey," replied Jack. "I suppose there's a dark side in all of us somewhere, waiting to come out."

"Sorry but I didn't get your name? I'm Jack by the way."

"It's okay there's no need for pleasantries, it was just one-night that's all. I'm happily married but wanted a change for once." As she got dressed and sat to do her hair, she giggled. "I suppose you could say we just committed adultery, how naughty is that?" smiling to herself as she turned on the hair dryer to dry her long blonde hair.

Jack took a shower to try and help sober up. 'Were last night's hallucinations real or all in my head like it used to be with the drugs before?' he said to himself. He decided it must have been his mind playing tricks fuelled by the drugs, thankful it was nothing more. After showering he returned to the bedroom, where his one-night stand was leaving as his phone rang. Leila's name was buzzing on the screen.

"Oh dear, the wife, is it? you can tell her that we only screwed for a few hours. I'm sure she'll understand, see yah." Smiling to him as she shut the door.

"Leila… where are you, I've been worried sick?"

"I just needed some time for myself. I was upset by your attitude; did you sign the documents in the end?'

"Err…Yes I did, why?"

She sighed. "Then it's done and there's no going back now, I wish you'd listened to my advice and walked away from the deal. But as your girlfriend, I'll stand by your side and support you." His necklace glowed once more, showing they were both connected again, and he could feel her love stronger than ever.

It was late afternoon by the time Reg finally appeared in the hotel reception, looking a little sheepish. After checking out, the pair made their way back to Liverpool Street and sat in an awkward silence. Both feeling embarrassed from the night before, not knowing how to break the silence. "Threesome, Reg, really?" said Jack jokingly, finally trying to make conversation.

"Ahem," was all Reg could muster, raising his eyebrows as he shook his paper to disappear behind it. The odd mutter under his breath then coming out every so often. "What a night, insatiable woman, weird man. Shaking his paper again as he turned to the next page. Giving a very a large "Ahhhemm," as he cleared his throat.

That Saturday evening Jack sat on his balcony with Leila watching the sun set. As the stars came out, she announced she'd received a call from her company, requiring her to spend a few days at a museum in Rome. Some old scrolls had been found hidden deep in their archive. They'd laid forgotten for hundreds of years and they wanted help in translating them if possible. She was heading off first thing Monday to catch a lunchtime flight and promised to bring him something nice back. They cosied up together for the rest of the weekend, spending as much time together as possible. They were now very deeply in love and hated being apart.

Monday came but Jack was nowhere to be seen and his cell was going straight to voicemail. Leila was already heading to the airport and her cell phone was off as well. Reg was frustrated they weren't answering, as he needed to know what he was doing about the consortium. The previous discussion had broken down without resolution and a final decision was still awaited.

"Well, Jack, how did the negotiations go, did you sell? Are you now a rich man?"

"Martin, he paid full price for the portfolio so yes, I'm now loaded and have a beautiful woman by my side. Life couldn't be better. All I need now, is for you guys to agree on our side of the deal?"

Martin took another mouthful of bacon and egg as he continued to listen. They were at a local café having an early morning breakfast meeting. Jack explained Lucifer was going to pay him to manage his old portfolio for a year in return for a hefty fee. On top of this he was going to employ him on a freelance basis. To secure some land acquisitions he wanted. This did include the warehouses as well, however.

Martin coughed and spluttered as his food went down the wrong way. Quickly gulping some tea to help wash it down properly.

"Are you completely bloody mad. You can't work for him and with us as well to secure the warehouses at the same time?"

"That's the beauty of it, mate. I have it in writing that I can only ever bid on his behalf up to £2million, not a penny more. You guys can bid slightly higher, so then hopefully, the rest of the competition is out bid as well." He took a big slurp of tea before continuing. "My cash will provide the holding deposit needed for a month, while the rest of you raise the rest of the capital to close the sale and release the deeds. It's a win, win situation."

Martin could sort of see the logic and accepted Jack had the guy under control but still raised another question. "What if he turns up and bids himself, he'll easily be able to go higher?"

"That won't happen, he spends a lot of time travelling and doesn't have the time spare. He wants someone he can trust to buy on his behalf, and he chose me. If he kicks off saying I should've bid higher; I can say our contract states, I don't have the authority… we can't lose!"

Martin nodded showing signs of understanding the logic and made a call to the rest of the consortium. After lots of mumbling, explaining, nodding, and waving of his free hand, he finally got off the phone. Acknowledging to Jack that they'd get back to him within a couple of hours. The pair shook hands as they parted, leaving Jack to head back to his flat to wait for the call. Back at his flat he placed his phone on charge as the battery was flat again and boiled the kettle.

He sat clock watching, then checking his phone every few minutes as it charged. Waiting for the screen to light up with that all-important call from the consortium. Two hours past with no response and needing something to take his mind off it, he started to have a tidy up. He dusted around the photos on the small table knocking the shoe box off. The cloth unfolded and the lid came off as it hit the floor, where the letter from his parents fell out.

Picking everything up he sat down looking at the half-opened envelope. Deciding to finally finish off what he'd started three years earlier he opened it. As he went to pull the letter out of the envelope, his phone rang he could see it was Martin calling back. Quickly pushing the letter back in, he placed it in the box again and answered the call.

"Hi, Jack, sorry about the wait. It's been a long morning and we needed time to discuss all risks and options collectively."

"I understand, have you reached a final decision yet?"

"Yes."

"And?" There were a few seconds of silence as Jack drummed his fingers nervously on the kitchen worktop.

"Well one the problem is, one of our members still doesn't like it and won't commit. We've therefore had to speak to our financiers again to see if we can move on without her."

"Oh, I take it that's a problem the rest of you, who pulled out?"

"It's Nena, Leila's old school friend. She just wouldn't come on board, saying she wasn't prepared to take the risk."

Jack sighed bracing himself for the worst.

"Well, the truth is, Jack, her decision places a huge financial strain on the rest of us now. You know and… well… despite all of that and after lots of talking, we think we can do it without her. Therefore, we're still in buddy!" Jack yelled with joy—his master plan was finally coming into force.

"That's great mate, I'll get onto Reg right now and meet you later today to finalise the paperwork," quickly ending the call to get hold of Reg.

"Reg, it's me."

"Where the hell have you been, I have been trying to call you all morning."

"Yeah, sorry, flat phone battery again. anyway, it's all on, the consortium's in and we need to meet them this afternoon to seal the deal. I'll pick you up in an hour from your office, we can talk on route."

"Wait, Jack, what… who… when are you… oh, he's hung up."

Chapter 10

Loyalties

Leila was back from her trip to Rome and working from her office once again. Leaving more time for the pair to spend together. That weekend they took a romantic trip to Paris and at the top of the Eiffel Tower she gave Jack a ring.

"What's this an ancient artefact that transports you from one place to another?" he asked jokingly.

"Not exactly darling, but it's said in old scrolls discovered, suggest that such a ring does exist, albeit it's never been found."

Leila looked at Jack lovingly and before he could say anything else she proposed. The crowd at the top of the viewing area clapped as they hugged and kissed. Jack couldn't believe it especially as it's usually the man that proposes.

Returning to his flat again late on the Sunday evening, a large envelope was waiting on the mat. Lucifer had sent some brochures through the post about the 1st lot of land he wanted him to get. Jack thought this would be a good opportunity to test a theory he had and before the auction started, put in a pre-auction bid of £1Million.

As the lot came up, he took his traditional position at the back of the room to watch. The consortium was also there watching, they too wanted to see Jacks theory being put to the test. The auctioneer started proceedings as normal, explaining the lot of land for sale and some of its history. There was plenty of mumbling, grunting, and nodding of heads as various factions undertook their usual pre-bid rituals and then he started.

This time however, he changed from his standard stance of "Who will start me at," instead beginning with "I have a pre-auction bid already on the table regarding this particular lot. I therefore must start proceedings toady at £500,000, which is above the guide price, am I bid more?" The room was full of gasps as people looked at each other in disbelief. A paddle came up, as a voice nervously put forward £550,000.

"I now have £550,000 from the floor, anymore. There's no bids from the internet, so it's all with you in the room." Another paddle was raised and £570,000 was nervously bid as the auctioneer looked around, scanning the room for more offers but it stayed silent.

"I'm afraid the current bid is still not enough to challenge the pre-auction offer. If there are no other bids then, are we done, I'm selling?" There was complete silence as the gavel came down. "Sold then for an undisclosed amount." There were more gasps and mumbling as the auctioneer made a note in his book.

The consortium was impressed his theory worked and looked across at him smiling. Jack raised a hand saying for them to stay where they were as he wanted to play-things down. As the auction finished, Lucifer's London team transferred the funds to the auction house and the deeds were released into Jack's care. Back at his flat later that evening Leila arrived for dinner. As they sat having a drink on his balcony, he decided to have a look at the deeds and see what was so special about the land.

Laying the information out across the dining table he began to have a look. From the aerial photographs he noticed scarring in the ground. The land must have been once used for more than just agriculture, suggesting a much older history. Leila followed the lines with her fingers and looked on her laptop checking her works data base.

"Yes," she said spinning the laptop round. Pointing to some translated text on the screen. She then pulled up some more history associated with the area. Homing in on a medieval map with further reference to a local myth.

She read the information on her screen out loud as it translated for her. "The land in medieval times was said to sit on ancient interconnecting ley lines. According to legend, it had once been a place of worship and sacrifice and the epicentre where the ley lines connected, holding a powerful energy force."

"What does that mean?" questioned Jack.

"Simply put a place of evil, even perhaps devil worship."

"Surely that's just fantasy, isn't it? What would Lucifer want with it now?"

"Well, my love, you did say he likes to collect the weirdest things, why not this as well?"

Lucifer of course was overjoyed when he received his prize and two more lots were duly put forward for him to secure. Jack was happy as well, he was on commission and the higher the bid, the richer, he was becoming. The next two lots were secured and again Leila lent a hand to help decipher their importance. Both of them viewing the deeds and the history together before handing them over to Lucifer. She soon discovered a similar pattern emerging. All three appeared to be interconnected by the same ley lines.

Jack couldn't work out the relevance, dismissing it as coincidence. Leila however lay her suspicions with the myth associated with ley lines. It was said in ancient readings that they carried an energy force, which spread itself around the world. The research she'd undertaken also referenced a battle that once took place in the area. Good and evil fighting for the power control of the ley lines, but as evil became overthrown, the devil was forced to flee.

To make sure it never returned, holy men had deep trenches cut through them. This then stopped the energy flow from meeting at the three interconnecting points. Further protecting the cuts by back filling them with a lining of lead, to prevent them from being reconnected. Pointing at the photos she advised that if repaired, where the scarring could be seen on the photos, the energy force could in essence be re-established.

Jack of course scoffed at the notion, saying it was nothing more than stuff and nonsense. Lucifer however was over the moon again. Shouting with joy when Jack handed the deeds over. Excitedly telling him to prepare for the warehouses as they were coming up in just a few weeks. Jack however was already prepared, in fact more than prepared.

With his commission and money from the sale of his portfolio, he'd amassed £1.7 million. More than enough to cover the holding deposit required if their plan worked. This also helped the consortium, as they were struggling to cover the shortfall with their lenders following Nena pulling out.

He carried on researching the warehouses in his spare time, reading all the information he'd gleaned and more. Trawling the internet and studying the ground investigations and other surveys available. Trying to see if the land was suitable for new housing or just stick with the warehouses as they were and sell on as a renovation opportunity. If the ground was contaminated and needed remediation, it's value would be affected. A brownfield site would be worth less compared to a greenfield site and would have to be reflected in the sell on price.

Leila was interested in the surveys as she'd never seen much in the way of this type before. She was only used to surveying ancient maps, studying aerial photos, or information gathered from test trenching with archaeological teams. He laid out the survey records of the land and levels, the existing services and GPS coordinates of the warehouses and boundaries.

The ground conditions looked good and the land itself was greenfield. Meaning the only remediation required was associated with the warehouses themselves. With no other major ecology problems to worry about, the warehouses and the land, would be much easier to sell on. With plenty of potential usage options available, they could command a much better sell on value in return.

While he continued reading through the information, Leila looked on her own laptop. Searching in her works archives against the coordinates provided from the surveys and gasped.

"Look…! the ley lines cross each other like I told you. When the three lots are plotted, they line up, forming a triangle and guess what's right in the middle?" Jack looked down and was astonished to see the warehouses sitting dead centre.

"I've already told you, Leila, it's just coincidence," he muttered to himself as he turned back to his documents. "It's just myth and legend as far as I'm concerned, I'm not interested in old wives' tales."

Leila pulled her necklace out from under her top and showed it to him. Reminding him they both wore something that was supposed to be nothing more than myth or legend, yet it was real.

"What if Lucifer really is evil, the devil even. If he gets hold of the warehouses, it would complete the triangle. If the ley lines were then reconnected, the powers epicentre would be right below them and you've purchased them on his behalf."

She tapped away again looking through her archives.

"Here," she said turning the laptop round and pointing at the screen. "The sign of devil worship, a triangular symbol with a dot in the middle. The ancient text translated from this old document warns of its danger. If an energy triangle can be established with a powerful enough energy force at its centre, a portal can be opened to the gates of hell. The ley lines, Jack, they have a natural energy flowing through them. They also form a triangle around the warehouses where they cross each other."

The colour drained from his face slightly as he looked at the screen. "Oh, Leila, come on. Mythical objects that are real are one thing but the devil... really? Lucifer likes to collect weird things that make no sense to anyone else. I've told you before, the guy's an eccentric and has underlined issues going on that's all."

They ended by agreeing Leila's own work obsession had perhaps allowed her mind to run wild and it was likely just a coincidence after all. Jack packed everything away and they settled on the sofa to watch some TV, when her phone rang. She rolled her eyes with displeasure as she pointed at the screen. Leila clearly had little time for the guy calling and Jack sniggered as he folded his arms to wait for what he had to say.

"Hi, Leila, have you heard the news?" almost shouting with excitement.

"No obviously not Arty. What's so important that it can't wait until the morning?"

"They've dug up something again near the Jordan River, this time in the actual riverbank. Artifacts apparently dating back to the time of Christ, a group of archaeologists are heading there right now. They want our team out there as well to try and help identify the finds and translate any documents found."

"Really?"

"Yeah… even our main benefactors going, we'll finally meet them for the first time, isn't it exciting. Apparently from the inscriptions found on pottery, part of a story is being told, which looks like it's about the birth of Christ, but they need us to help work it out."

Leila however wasn't so impressed; she'd just got engaged and wanted to spend time with her finance. Not trudge around the mud and muck of a riverbank. It would be hot and muggy, full of midges and possibly disease ridden as well. Jack was also worried for her safety he didn't want her to go either. after reassurance the team would be looked after and protected, he felt a bit happier. She also reminded him that if there was no phone signal, they could still share their thoughts and feelings through their necklaces.

Selfishly he wanted her to be with him at the auction but realised that duty to her job had to take precedence. After all, she was the best in her field and her team needed her. The next morning, he drove her to Heathrow to meet up with the rest of her colleagues. After a few hugs and kisses, the team said their goodbyes and walked through the main doors to the terminal. Laughing and chatting excitedly, leaving Jack with the other loved ones standing in the rain waving them off.

The drive back home for Jack was painfully slow and arduous. The rain had caused a huge accident on the motorway, adding hours of delays just to add to his torment. He spent the time thinking about Leila, who would now be boarding the plane. The amazing experiences she was about to have, unlocking more secrets from the past. Then his thoughts drifted to his family, no longer alive to see him finally get engaged and become a wealthy man.

His mind wandered back to the past, his parents and brother, his grandparents, and the hidden life that they seemed to have kept from him. Who was the hooded figure in the grounds at Mount St Michael, perhaps he should visit again while she was away? His phone suddenly started to ring, breaking the silence—it was Reg.

"Hi, Jack, did Leila get away okay?"

"Yes, Reg, thanks for asking, what's up?"

"Oh good... good, I just wondered if you were free for supper tonight, I could do with the company."

"Sure, I'll book us a table in town, shall I pick you up from your house around seven thirty?"

"Yes, that would be good."

"Are you okay, Reg, you don't sound yourself?"

"Yes, I'm fine, Jack, thanks for asking... see you later."

Jack could tell he wasn't himself as he hung up, but just thought he needed some company. He called Reg's favourite restaurant, booked a table, and continued heading home to get changed.

Reg was already waiting on the doorstep when he arrived, looking very troubled. He got in without saying a word choosing to wait until Jack drove away before he spoke. "Are you scared of death?"

"What sort of bloody question is that, are you okay Reg, the colour's drained from your cheeks, is something troubling you, you're not ill, are you?"

"Do you remember in London at Lucifer's offices when I said, I saw my own death."

"Sort of—why? what's up?"

"I somehow feel I won't be around for much longer."

"I don't know what's got into you today old man, but you'll live to see me out you've always looked after yourself, I haven't."

136

The pair arrived in town and after parking they started to make their way to the restaurant when Jack's phone pinged.

"Ah… its Leila, they've landed and are heading to the hotel for a briefing," he scrolled down the screen to read the rest of the text. "Typical… the archaeologists have already uncovered more artefacts, so they're being briefed to expect staying longer than the initial two weeks."

"Have you spoken to Lucifer recently?"

"What… no, I only speak to him when I have to—why?"

"I was just wondering if he was about that's all."

"I think he's in the country currently but then he's away on business why?"

"Oh, just wondered that's all."

"For Fuck's sake, Reg, what's up with you today. Come on let's get a few drinks down you and put the world to rights."

The pair had their meal and following plenty of bottles of beer, made their way to a bar for a few more. Reg was still on edge, drinking solidly but Jack couldn't snap him out of his depressed state. They continued drinking and chatting, but every time Reg started to relax, he'd change again. Anxiously looking around the bar to see who else was there.

Leaning in drunkenly towards Jack, he whispered. "Do you know, your parents and grandparents would be so proud of what you've achieved. Especially with Leila, she's beautiful."

"Thanks, mate that means a lot."

"When your time comes make sure you do it with honour and valour," slapping him on his shoulder.

"Come on old man you're talking in riddles now, time to get you home I think."

He helped his old friend up out of his chair and out into the main street to hail a taxi. The driver turned as Jack put a seat belt around him. "He'd better not puke mate, or I'll have to charge extra to clear the mess up." Jack nodded advising that there was plenty of money in it for him to drive his old friend home and drop him back as well.

Dropping Reg off first he watched him struggling to open his front door. Missing the lock every time he went to put his key in. Jack got out of the taxi to help as the cab driver was filming his antics and laughing. Once inside he asked if he needed help to get upstairs but Reg refused. Adamant, he just wanted to sit in his favourite chair in the lounge. So, Jack helped him sit down and placed a blanket over his lap to keep him warm. Although he still looked anxious, he wanted to be left where he was and bid him a good night. Jack then left, saying he'd catch up with him in the morning.

It was around two in the morning when Reg was first awakened. A bang outside startled him, waking him from his drunken slumber. He got up to have a look but soon settled again after realising cats were fighting, and the bins had gone over. He was woken again at three, this time hearing strange noises outside. Like hyenas laughing and strange whispers calling out his name.

A cold shiver raced through his body as he began breathing more anxiously. A thin mist started to spread into his lounge and a figure appeared walking through it. He could make out a head tilting from side to side as a man moved towards him, wiping his mouth across one of his suit sleeves.

"Hi, Reg, guess it's judgement day my old friend. Is the scene familiar, just as I'd planted it in your mind?"

Reg clasped his hands tightly together and placed them on his lap to wait his fate in silence.

"Have you pieced it all together old man, have you worked

it all out?"

Reg nodded but stayed quiet. "Clever boy… I've no further need for you now then; you've served your purpose." Pulling out his whip and starting to swing it around his head. Tiny blue flecks started to appear, growing longer and longer until strands of lightning could be seen.

Reg was terrified but still sat with his hands firmly clasped together as he stared back. Lucifer's face now lit up by the blue light, transformed into a terrifying looking beast. Pulling the whip back, he cracked it forwards, sending the strands out at him. Gripping tightly around his body, he could feel its forces pulling hard at his soul from deep inside.

He shook violently as it was ripped from his body, leaving his lifeless husk sat upright in his chair. As the threads retracted, Lucifer calmly slicked his hair back and briefly looked in the mirror. He watched his reflection transform back to his human self and with a quick twist of the ring on his finger he vanished.

The next morning Jack was up late, nursing a raging hangover. After having breakfast and a long shower, he made his way back into town to pick up his Range Rover. He'd stupidly forgotten to get an overnight parking ticket and was met with a yellow pouch stuck to the windscreen. Tearing it from under the wipers, he found an unwelcome £50 fine tucked inside, 'just great' he thought to himself. He was still grumbling as he drove past Reg's house. The curtains weren't open so he thought he must be still sleeping his own hangover off.

He spent the rest of the day checking on his old houses, making sure the tenants had no issues before starting his journey home. Driving along the dual carriageway his phone rang and he touched the button on the dashboard screen to answer.

"Hello… Jack Skye?"

"Hi, Jack, its Reg's business partner here Greg Matthews."

"Oh, hi Greg how are you and your wife, I haven't heard from you in a while. I bet Reg hasn't shown up for work, has he? he's probably still at home sleeping it off, he had a lot to drink last night, and his curtains were still drawn when I drove past earlier."

"Jack, I'm sorry to have to say this, but Reg is dead. We found him dead earlier, the police are with me now."

Jack swerved almost hitting the central reservation, as he lost concentration for a second. "What did you say?" straightened up again after being beeped at by another car. "Hang on I'll call you straight back, I'm just coming up to some services… give me two minutes." He was distraught as he pulled in, quickly coming to a flying halt and pressing redial.

"Thanks for calling straight back, Jack. He never showed up for work today, so we used the spare key in the office to check on him. We found him dead in his chair."

"Are you sure he's dead, he was only with me last night, what happened?"

"The police officer who attended with the ambulance crew wants to talk to you, hold on."

"Mr Skye, my names officer Stanway, sorry to speak in such difficult circumstances, but are you able to come straight to the station please. We've some questions to ask to try and help us piece things together."

"Erm sure, okay… I'll turn around straight away, I can be there in… say, forty minutes?"

"Thank you, that's helpful, just ask for me at the station desk on arrival."

He sped back to town where he was met by two officers and led to an interview room. "Thanks for coming Mr Skye, we have some questions to ask about your movements last night." Jack said he had nothing to hide and was glad to help in any way he could. He explained the previous day's events, the strange phone call he'd received from Reg. Asking to have dinner with him and noticing he was off colour and nervous all night.

He talked about what they had to eat and the bar they went to for further drinks. The cab journey home, dropping him off on the way and having to help inside the house as he was so drunk. He explained about offering to help put him to bed, but how adamant he was to just sit in his favourite chair in the lounge. After placing a blanket over his lap to keep him warm he left, saying he would see him in the morning.

The officer then seeming happy enough with his responses. Advising his death wasn't being treated as suspicious. They did however have to ask him about something they'd found in Reg's hands. Three photos were placed on the table and Jack stared at them in horror. He was sitting bolt upright, just as he'd left him with his blanket over his lap. Only his hands were clasped together with what looked like a piece of paper sticking out from between his fingers.

His face looked to be etched with terror, as though he'd died of fright. Initially he looked away, finding the photos too shocking to look at, then looked again more closely. "How did he die?" he asked.

"We're still trying to piece that together, but we're sure it was probably a massive heart attack, the autopsy will clarify. It's the note that we found that we want to talk to you about, can you explain what this means?" as the scrunched paper was opened out on the table.

He picked it up, noticing it was scruffily written, as though in a rush.

'All isn't as it seems be careful.'

He had no idea what it meant but the questions kept coming.

"Have you known Mr Philips long Mr Skye?"

"Yes, he's been my family's lawyer for years, he was like a father figure to me in the end. We became very close friends; he's been alongside me ever since I first started property developing."

After answering even more questions, it was late afternoon by the time the officers said they had no further questions and he was free to go. Eliminated from any further investigations he made his way out and sobbed deeply when he got back in his car. He couldn't believe his friend was gone and what was he trying to tell him with the message. He left the Police station and headed straight home. Sinking his sadness into a bottle of red, he sat listening to his chill out music while staring at the photos he was asked to cherish.

Chapter 11

Messages from Beyond

Leila had been away for over eight days and the only means of communication was via their necklaces. There was no mobile signal at the dig site, and they were only returning to the hotel every few days. Jack told her when she was back at the hotel that Reg was gone, after suffering a massive heart attack. She was also deeply upset to hear the news. She'd grown fond of Reg and knew how close he and Jack had become over the years. She wished she could be there to support him and was sorry she couldn't. She let him know that she was safe and that she loved and missed him dearly.

She talked about work to take his mind off Reg, saying it was interesting yet strange. Testing all known theories about the time of Christ but couldn't expand further due to its sensitivity. He wished they could talk longer, but she had to go as her transport was waiting to take her back to the dig. She would be in touch soon but had to go again for now. Saying she loved him, she wished him good luck with the forthcoming auction. As the line went dead, his necklace slowly dimmed until dull again, as their mind connections separated.

The big auction was now only a week away, but Lucifer was still hanging around, putting Jack on edge. He was paranoid he'd show up and bid for the warehouses himself, until eventually getting the call he was waiting for. He was going to be away on business and wouldn't be able to attend. After placing all confidence in Jack to secure the warehouses, he said his goodbyes leaving him to it. A meeting was then quickly arranged with the consortium at their conference centre, to run through final preparations. They too were also sorry to hear the news that Reg had died and could tell it had hit Jack very hard, despite him trying to carry on regardless.

With the auction so close, he wanted to go through the details one last time. This would be the final chance to see them before the auction itself. Plus, he was also busy organising Reg's funeral arrangements. The tactic would be the same as the first land lot where he tested his theory. A pre-auction bid of £1 million would be placed so that lucifer thought he was bidding seriously for him.

The consortium would then bid quickly, taking the bids to £1.8 million before slowing down again. It would then be a slow tussle building up to £2 million where he'd then stop. Leaving the consortium to counter, hopefully seeing off the rest of the competition in the final stages.

Following the meeting, he rushed back home; Leila was due back at her hotel. They could talk again properly instead of communicating with their necklaces. He sat on his balcony waiting for her to video call and was relieved to finally see her face and hear her voice again. He asked how the work was going to which she replied very well, but it was still too sensitive to discuss from the hotel. The repercussions would be serious if their findings were to be leaked out.

She also had some further news, "Guess what our main private benefactor's here, he's the most charming of guys and what's more he knows you as well."

"Oh?" queried Jack.

"Yeah… he's taking us all out to dinner, here he is now in fact, come and say hi to my fiancé, Jack."

A familiar voice was heard giving him goosebumps, "Hi Jack, how's it going?"

"Lucifer, I thought you were away on business?"

"I am, I support these people financially and when they find something of interest, I get first dibs on adding it to my collection. What's being discovered here is fascinating, so I had to come. The public must never know what's been discovered, it could change world history and religion as we know it. It's much better in my hands where it can be kept safe."

"Anyway, nice talking, got to go now. I'm verry much looking forward to getting to know your future wife better while I'm here." Giving him a wink before walking out of the phones video shot.

Jack wasn't at all happy but had no choice but to trust Leila wouldn't be fooled by his deceptive mind games. She called him again later that night, saying they would be out of signal range for the next few days, so they'd have to rely on their necklaces to communicate again temporarily.

The next three days were murder for him, Leila couldn't communicate when she wanted to. She didn't want the others to know the necklaces were once part of a mythological antiquity and Jack certainly didn't want Lucifer finding out. It glowed too brightly at night in their tents, and it was difficult during the day. There was little privacy as the team were working in a tight compounded area with armed guards watching all the time.

In the interim, Jack tried to keep himself busy. Reg was going to be cremated the day after the auction and he'd already placed a pre-auction bid of £1 million on Lucifer's behalf. He'd also notified the team in London to prepare the funds in readiness for him to bid up to £2 million.

He'd also received a few sneaky photos of the dig area where Leila was. She'd found at certain times of the day she could get a one bar signal for just a few seconds near the toilet tents. Although as unsanitary as it was, it did enable her to send the odd text or photo.

The area looked like a military operation, high solid fencing with armed guards sitting on top of ladder towers. Reminding him of the one's lifeguards used in swimming pools. Clearly there to protect the work force, while other photos showed guards posted around the tents where the accommodation was and where the antiquities were being worked upon.

It looked hot, dusty, and uninviting but for Leila's team they were well used to working in harshness. Where the river meandered, looked like part of its embankment had been removed where the main dig was happening. The river was low for the time of year and the photo must have been taken with her standing in it, just up from the dig, so that she could fit it all into the shot.

Although the photos were intriguing, they didn't give much else away and none showed any of the findings. He knew they were unearthing things that could potentially rewrite history, but he really wanted to know what. He understood she couldn't send photos with or discuss any of the findings in detail, which frustrated him. He did like her selfie however, showing her in her works outfit. Cream-coloured shorts, white socks, brown working boots and a white vest top. Over the top she wore a cream shirt that was undone and tied in a knot at the front, capped off with a wide brimmed hat. She looked like a character out of an Indiana Jones movie which made him chuckle.

Finally, on the third day she was back at the hotel for a break, but said they were far from finished. She couldn't hold back her excitement any longer and gushed what they'd found. A skeleton had been discovered but it was very unusual. Slightly disformed, mostly human but also slightly animal-like. At first discovery the archaeologists thought it was a human buried with an animal. It had clearly been killed as a hand and wrist were missing, severed in one blow by a sharp blade. It was unclear if it was a ritual killing or something more sinister, as there were no other signs of trauma indicating a main cause of death. Either way an extension to the dig permit had been requested so that they could investigate further.

She asked how the funeral plans were going and he told her he'd managed to get a crematorium booking for the day after the auction. He was going round to Reg's house in the morning to meet the company clearing it. He was also arranging for the deeds to be passed onto Reg's business partner, so the house could be sold on. The money would then be split between the practices loyal staff who'd been there with Reg and Greg since the beginning. He felt Reg would have liked that and Leila agreed it was a lovely gesture.

She noticed he appeared tired, asking how he was in himself. He was feeling lonely, and sad his friend was gone and his finance was thousands of miles away. She held her palm to the screen of the phone asking him to do the same. His necklace glowed brightly as though their palms were touching for real. He felt her love flowing between them and he missed her dearly, wishing he could be with her.

There was a sudden knock at her hotel room door, and she grumbled at being rudely interrupted. It was one of her female companions shouting from the corridor. Her voice muffled slightly behind the door.

"Come on dozy, Lucifer will be waiting for us downstairs," she knocked again more loudly before shouting. "See you down there then."

"Sorry," she said, "I've got to go," sighing deeply. "I'll give you a call tomorrow to see how the house clearance went… love you, Jack," and once more he was on his own.

Morning came and he headed straight for Reg's house to meet the house clearers. He wandered around from room to room, trying to picture how he'd have gone about his daily routines. It was strange being in the house again and although a reasonably wealthy chap, Reg had the simplest of tastes. Living with outdated furniture and fittings more akin with the early eighties.

The house clearers walked around with him, making an itinerary of what they'd keep and what they'd throw. "You okay with the twelve-yard skip out front mate, most of this will probably go straight to land fill to be honest," Jack nodded replying it was fine.

The silence in the street then broken by the skip lorry reversed into the front driveway. Chains clanging and clattering as the lorry lifted the skip off settling, it on the ground before driving off again. The supervisor of the gang then called his men into action. "Right, lads, let's get this stuff sorted. All the shit goes in the skip and the decent stuff gets loaded into the Luton van parked in the street. Here's the itinerary, now shake a leg, we've another clearance booked this afternoon."

Jack continued walking around the ground floor rooms. Pondering why Reg appeared to be staring straight ahead in the photos the police showed him. He sat in the armchair trying to work it out. Why write a cryptic note and die sitting bolt upright, staring forwards. He looked up at the mirror above the fireplace and stood up, wondering if there something hidden there. He walked across to the mantlepiece to look for any clues but there was nothing. He removed the mirror and looked on the back but again there was nothing.

He held it close to his face looking at the edges. Trying to see if the clasps holding it to its backing had been removed but no, it was just a standard art deco mirror. Hanging it back up he suddenly noticed his breath had made something stand out. He went into the kitchen and found a can of furniture polish under the sink and gently sprayed it across its face at an angle.

A message appeared written using a finger, 'The devil is in disguise trust no-one,' he shuddered as he read it; what was he trying to tell him? Was Lucifer really the devil in disguise or was someone in the consortium. Maybe Martin or even Nana, after all she didn't want to be part of the deal, and Martin certainly seemed to know far too much for his own good.

He jumped as the house clearer walked into the room, his face suddenly appearing in the mirror. "Sorry mate didn't mean to startle you… when we've finished shall we drop the keys back at the solicitors if that works for you?"

"Sure," he said wiping the mirror clean and straightening it on the wall. He called Reg's business partner as he left, relaying the message that the house clearers would drop the keys back when they were finished. Putting the furniture polish back under the sink, he left and made his way back home to his flat.

It was now the night before the auction as he paced anxiously around his flat, trying to keep himself calm and controlled. His phone had been ringing non-stop with regards to Reg's funeral arrangements, but the call he wanted the most hadn't come. Leila hadn't called to see how the house clearance had gone and he was worried that Lucifer was with her.

He played over and over in his mind how the auction might

go, trying to see if there were any details he hadn't thought about when his phone lit up, it was Leila.

"Thank God, it's you. I've been stressing out all evening worrying about where you are?"

"Oh, don't worry about us we're just hauled up in the hotel until the paperwork for extending the dig is sorted out. We've been chilling out by the pool all day and lost track of time. Lucifer's such a card."

"He says you've got a wild side to you when you're out, that you're a completely different person, what does he mean by that?"

"Nothing he's just winding you up, he likes to get inside people's heads, he gets off on it. Just ignore him and whatever you do, please be careful around him, he's slippery."

They talked about her day, how she'd got sun burnt after falling asleep, following a heavy lunchtime session. How one of her female colleagues had been caught coming out of Lucifer's bedroom looking rather flushed. Jack didn't have that sort of gossip to share, he could only talk about the house clearance and the auction in the morning. She joked he sounded like a boring middle-aged man but promised they'd go somewhere special when she returned. Having to then cut the call short as she was late for a meeting with the rest of the team.

He felt rejected again, she was having a great time and spending less and less time talking to him. He was sad and gloomy, with his future hanging in the balance. He filled a glass with red wine and opened the door to his balcony to watch the sunset. But it was now raining, forcing him to sit inside and watch TV instead.

Chapter 12

False Pretences

Beep, beep, beep, beep, beep. A hand slammed down onto the alarm clock. It was five in the morning and Jack needed to be up and alert. Instead, he was hungover and didn't want to get up. He dragged himself out of bed, got changed and headed out for a 5K run to shake off the spider's webs in his head, stopping for a quick takeaway Latte on his way back.

Back at his flat he started to feel more alert and after showering and having breakfast, put on his best suit ready for the day ahead. A text came in from Martin, 'Good luck today buddy see you there, we're behind you.' His suspicious mind kicked in again. Was this who Reg was warning about? He sat on his balcony having another coffee when Leila video called. "Hi Hun," Waving at the camera. "Hope you're okay and good luck for today... knock 'em all dead."

She sounded very jolly and touching his necklace, he could see hers glowing back. "I won't be able to call you until tomorrow now. We're heading back to the site to box some of our findings and get them sent to a safer place. See you later, love you, byeeeee." She gave a quick wave and blew a kiss then cut off. He was happy she'd taken the time to call to wish him luck and his confidence grew inside again. After brushing his teeth and putting on some aftershave, he grabbed his keys and headed out.

All the way down the motorway he kept receiving calls from friends and other people, about the plans for the funeral the next day. He gave the details of the crematorium, saying there'd also be a wake at the pub just down from Reg's offices. He was already feeling hassled, and still had an hour's drive in front of him to get to the auction rooms.

Pulling in at some services he took a quick comfort break and got a take-away latte, pastry, and a black coffee. Getting back into his Range Rover, he went to pass the coffee over before realising Reg was no longer there.

He laughed to himself realising his mistake. He was so used to him being there that over time, it'd become synonymous to simply buy him a coffee every time he stopped at any services. He sat the coffee in its usual holder on the passenger's side and raised his latte, "Here's to you, old man." Taking a large sip before clearing his throat with a large, "Ahh hemm." He laughed loudly as he pulled away. "Bloody hell, Reg… I'm turning into you now."

Mid-morning finally arrived, and he was in position at the back of the auction room, watching the competition enter. The consortium walked in without paying him any attention just as planned. Separating as they went in to stand in different locations in the room. There were lots of different people that he didn't recognise which he'd predicted. It was a much more exclusive group, more akin with a premier league rather the championship league he'd been used to dealing in.

The auctioneer started the smaller land lots first, which were quickly snapped up for low prices by self-builders and small developers. Houses came next with Jack spotting a few good potentials, but he couldn't bid as he needed his money for the holding deposit, if they won.

A short half an hour break was announced and as people scuttled out for comfort breaks, he looked upwards. Silently praying his plan would come off, just as his phone buzzed in his pocket. It was a text from Reg's phone, 'Get the auction done, sell on and disappear as quickly as you can, you're not safe.' He looked at it in amazement, 'how can Reg be texting, he's dead,' he said to himself as it buzzed again. 'Sorry, just turned Reg's phone on to check it. He had a message in his outbox that hadn't sent, and I couldn't stop it sending, sorry about that—Greg Matthews.' He breathed a sigh of relief, but again didn't understand what was with the cryptic messages were about, that was the third one now.

The room started to fill again and after a few minutes, the atmosphere was loud and buzzing again, in anticipation of the big-ticket items. The auctioneer started again, "Thank you ladies and gentlemen, now onto the main event, lot 72 the sale of warehouses and associated land. A nice lot this, the warehouses date back to the late 1800's, when first used as workhouses before later turned into factories after the second world war."

He looked around the room, stared at the screen with the internet bidders on and continued.

"There's been a lot of interest in these, and we've had quite a few pre-auction bids placed already." Jack swallowed hard, he'd not anticipated that and felt a bit stupid. Martin gave a brief glance from the middle of the crowd, as if to say the same, before turning away again.

"On the foundation of the pre-auction bids received and the interest we have on the internet today, I'll start proceedings at £1.2 Million." He was relieved it wasn't higher, he thought it was going to be much more based on what he'd said.

The auctioneer continued:

"I now have a bid on-line for £1.25 Million, it's with you in the room, who'll bid me £1.5 Million?" A paddle was quickly raised, then another, this time for £1.75 Million. Jack now joined in, putting in a bid for Lucifer at £1.8 Million.

The auctioneer checked his screen. "It's still currently in the room at £1.8 Million, we've no further bids presently on the internet."

£1.85 Million was offered from another new bidder, a further counter bid then came in from the internet at £1.87 Million. Jack stood firm waiting as the auctioneer carried on. "We have £1.89 million now online, anymore from the room?"

Another paddle was raised as £1.9 million was bid. It was the consortium they were now starting to bid. The auctioneer checked his screen again and there were no counter bids.

"£1.9 million with you in the room then anymore?" a further bid was raised in the room for £1.92 Million.

"£1.95 million," came another voice, this time it was Martin's turn to chip in. Jack now struck again, raising his paddle for Lucifer with a counter bid of £1.97 million. The bids were becoming serious, and he could hear the gasps and whispers in the room as the pressure mounted.

Another bid came in on-line. "Ladies and gentlemen, we have a new bidder at £1.98 Million from the internet, it's with you again in the room."

"£1.99 million" was shouted, it was the consortium again. Jack felt it was time to finish it off and hit again.

"£2.0 million," he shouted raising his paddle aloft, the room filled with more gasps. He knew he couldn't do any more and Lucifer couldn't complain that he hadn't honoured his side of the contract.

"I'm now bid £2.1 million on the internet, anymore in the

room?" Jack started sweating, he thought that by now people would be backing off or perhaps it was Lucifer, bidding online from his hotel.

"£2.2 million" came from a new paddle, it was Samantha. Another consortium member who looked over-excited at placing a bid. The auctioneer checked his screen again before looking back across the room.

"Ladies and gentlemen, I'm now bid £2.4 million on the internet, it's back with you." The room was buzzing, a low murmuring could be heard as the sound of voices started to rise, Jack knew that his group were almost at their limit. £2.45 million was countered by the consortium, only to be pushed back with a further bid from the internet, at £2.47 million.

Martin looked over to Jack and he nodded back to counter. He put his paddle up for the final time shouting "£2.5 million." That was it they were all in with their contingency thrown in as well. The internet was silent, the room was silent, and the countdown began.

"Lot 72, warehouses and associated land going once at £2.5 million pounds… anymore in the room are we all done now?" he checked the internet. "Going twice then at £2.5 million… for the third and final time, all done then," bang went the gavel, and it was sold. They'd triumphed and Jack breathed a huge sigh of relief. He headed off to the main office and laid down his £1.7 million holding deposit. Giving the consortium four weeks to come up with the remaining £800,000, to complete on the sale enabling the deeds to be released.

The group then headed to a local pub to for celebratory drinks and discuss strategy before heading back. They advised they were meeting their lenders first thing in the morning and their conference centre would be used as collateral. Nena who'd dropped out, wasn't going to be made aware as the warehouses would be quickly sold on, therefore it was decided she didn't need to know.

Leila was simply overjoyed for Jack when she called that evening and couldn't believe he was going to be wealthier than he already was. He was sitting on his balcony, drinking champagne, and beaming with happiness. She touched her necklace and they both glowed brightly, he could feel how proud she was of him.

"Do I hear Celebrations; someone must have some good news?" came a familiar voice. Lucifer was in ear shot and Leila hadn't realised.

"Yes… Jack's just secured some warehouses and land at auction today."

He asked if he could speak to him, then noticed her necklace glowing gently. Hooking it with his fingers, he lifted it to have a look. "Interesting jewellery?" looking at it before letting it go as the phone was handed over. He looked at the screen, tilting his head slightly, noticing Jack's necklace was also glowing. Slicking his hair back with his other free hand, he was clearly trying to process what the necklaces did.

"How much did it cost then me in the end then, Jackee boy?"

"Sorry but you didn't win… I was outbid at £2 Million, and the lot finally went for £2.5 Million. There was nothing more I could do."

"I put a stake in with a consortium, that went on to win, so the celebrations about me not you."

Lucifer's eyes turned red with rage as his face almost started to transform, before stopping again. His eyes then turning blue again as his face turned back to normal. Throwing the phone back to Leila, he walked off waving his arms around in anger as he stomped back towards the hotel. "Someone's not happy?" she said. "He's walked off like a stroppy kid having a hissy fit."

They laughed at his antics, before Jack told her not to worry about him anymore. Once the lot was sold on, they could focus on getting married and having a perfect life. Knowing they'd be financially secure. Leila couldn't wait and hoped her work would soon finish so they could be together again, she hated being apart from him.

They continued to talk about Reg's funeral in the morning and how he wished he could have been there to see him win, raising his glass in respect to him. Leila hoped the day would go well, before saying sadly that she had to go. After their goodbyes he continued to sit outside, watching the stars in the night sky. As he toasted Reg again, a shooting star shot across the sky, burning up in the upper atmosphere and he took it as a good omen.

The next day the funeral went very well. Jack had found the best funeral celebrant he could find, and Reg had a good send-off. Ending in the local pub just down from his offices, where his staff and business partner had laid on a lavish spread.

The day then ended with Reg's business partner making an announcement. He and Jack had agreed the money raised from the sale of his house, would be equally shared between his staff. As a special thank you for their years of loyal service to him. There was barely a dry eye in the house as he finished.

Chapter 13

You Reap What You Sow

Three weeks had passed since the auction and Reg's funeral. Despite their efforts the consortium was still busy trying to raise the £800,000 needed. The earlier lender had decided to withdraw the loan offer, leaving them to find another lender. While this was going on, Jack decided to take a few days off and travelled back down to Cornwall. Leila was also back at the dig site and wouldn't be in contact again for a week, so he felt the break would do him some good. Recent events and weeks had drained on him, and he needed a recharge.

He headed along the coastline, taking in the places he previously visited with Leila and wondered at its beauty. Yet, he felt himself being drawn St Michaels Mount again. So, on a wet windy afternoon he sat in his Range Rover looking out across at it. It was high tide with no boats were travelling across, due to the stormy conditions. The want to be there seemed to run deep but he also needed to be back home. So, as he was unable to visit, he decided to plan a return trip once the warehouses were safely secured.

Since the auction there had been no management issues with his old housing stock and there were no further requirements from Lucifer either. With nothing to fill his time, he'd suddenly become slightly lazy. Drinking most nights, going to bed late and waking up late as there wasn't much else to keep his mind occupied.

The consortium had finally secured the funding they needed. The conference centre deeds were to be handed over as collateral at the end of the week and the loan would be finalised. Thankfully this was just in time as the holding period for the warehouses was nearly up. If they did not complete within the four-week holding period, Jack would lose his deposit and be left bankrupt.

His mood was also at a new low as Leila had stopped talking to him. Lucifer had let slip that Jack had slept with another man's wife in London, while celebrating the sale of his portfolio. He'd explained it was a drunken mistake. Lucifer had spiked his drinks and enticed him to take drugs, but she was very upset and deeply hurt by it all.

In response he'd had hit the bottle hard, stressing about completing on the warehouses in time and feeling depressed not having Reg around anymore. He was also angry that Lucifer used a cheap shot in revenge for not securing the warehouses for him.

He hadn't set his alarm again before going to bed that night, so didn't wake until well past nine the next morning. Sleepily walking to his kitchen, he put some bread in the toaster and set about making a cup of tea.

He switched the TV on while it brewed and sat at his breakfast bar taking some headache tablets. The local news was on, and a correspondent stood giving a live link broadcast. She was by a familiar looking road that overlooked some grounds. Blue lights were flashing in the background and recognising the area, he turned the volume up as he finished making his tea.

"I'm standing here this morning by the grounds of this old stately home here in the heart of Suffolk. Behind me his lovely old building, was only lovingly and beautifully restored a year ago and turned into a conference centre. The popular and successful group that own and run this old converted stately home are on its knees this morning, as fire ravaged through it in the early hours."

"Twelve fire crews were here at the height of the blaze, fighting to bring it under control but were unable to and the building has been completely gutted. Behind me three fire crews remain here this morning, damping down and making safe before investigations can begin to establish what the probable cause could have been."

"Early rumours indicate possible arson, with sources telling me this would place a huge financial burden on the owners if the insurers were to refuse to pay out. Bringing into doubt whether this beautiful old building will ever be saved again or if it will ever re-open."

"This beautiful old building had been lovingly transformed into a plush conference centre. It had become a very successful locally run business, bringing plenty of jobs to the local community at the same time."

"The lives and livelihoods of the consortium that owns and operates it and the local community that rely on it for their jobs, lays in tatters this morning, just like the building behind me."

"Angela Stephens... Anglia News... Bury St Edmunds... Suffolk."

He couldn't believe what he was seeing and hearing. The consortiums conference centre was nothing more than a pile of smoking rubble. It was supposed to be used as collateral to secure the £800,000 funding for the warehouses. If they couldn't raise the money, he faced financial ruin. He nervously picked up his phone to call Martin, but the battery was flat again. Cursing himself he put it on charge, quickly showered, dressed, and wrestled with his jacket, while eating the cold toast he'd forgotten about.

He ran down to his Range Rover and spun off heading for the conference centre. Plugging his phone charger into the USB port he turned his phone on. *Beep beep... beep beep... beep beep... beep beep... beep beep* the text messages and missed call notifications flew in as he frantically drove along. He called Martin but he wasn't picking up, so he left him a voicemail then listened to his own messages.

"You have five new messages,"

"First new message received today at 02.45 hours," *beep*— he could hear sirens in the background, it was Martin. "Jack, where are you? It's a bloody mess, the centres on fire and it's all going up in smoke... the fire's raging it's terrible."

"Next new message received today at 03.30 hours," *beep*— "Jack, it's Martin again for fucks sake pick up, where are you?" he could hear the anxiousness in his voice.

"Next new message received today at 04.00 hours," *beep*— "Jack, they've lost control, the fires really raging now it's all ruined, everything's ruined they're pushing us back for safety."

"Next new message received today at 04.45 hours," *beep*— a crashing noise could be heard. "Oh my god the roofs just gone in its shocking... where are you Jack... Jack... shit!"

"Next new message received today at 05.15 hours," *beep*— he could hear someone talking to Martin in the background, "What, oh God, no... you're kidding me... there's still someone in there... we've got to get them out... tell the Fire fighters quickly!"

"End of messages."

Jack put his foot down and thrashed along the motorway to get there as quickly as he could. He had no idea what he was walking into, but he had to be there to support his friends.

Screeching to a halt on the road outside the lavish gardens, he jumped out to see what was going on. The scene looked like a bomb had hit, destroying everything in its wake. The grand old building was now a burned-out shell, with piles of rubble strewn around. The walls had collapsed under the shear intensity of the heat, making the roof caved in on itself. Plumes of smoke were still rising from inside the shell as the fire crews continued dowsing down, keeping it from re-igniting.

He looked around and saw a small group with blankets wrapped round them, talking to the police and the chief fire officer. They were within a cordoned off area delineated by Police tape. He could see Samantha in floods of tears as he slowly made his way towards them but was stopped by a police officer.

"Sir, this is not a public area turn around and leave, it's not safe."

"It's okay, officer, he's with us, you can let him through." It was Martin. Jack stood taking in the devastation, as he looked around at what was left of the building. He could see film and radio crews on standby, ready to give their next bulletins. Standing on the path outside and recognised the reporter he'd seen earlier on the TV.

Martin filled him in on events as he knew them, "Just before two a.m. the off-site security monitoring station notified the CCTV had gone into operation, after one of the sensors tripped in the building. They recorded a man that appeared from nowhere who proceeded to the main hall."

"He ripped down some of the long curtains from the windows and piled them up in the middle of the floor, before doused them in petrol. The cameras then showed him walking around the rest of the ground floor, leaving petrol trails as he went. The monitoring station called the police and as they arrived, he was seen on the cameras making a phone call, before striking a match and throwing it onto the curtains."

"The curtains went up in a fire ball, including the petrol trails trapping the person inside. The cameras picked him up trying to shield his face from the inferno. He then disappeared as the cameras failed, it's unknown if the arsonist got out or not."

The news crews continued to report live every half hour as events unfolded. Picking up on rumours that a search for a body was being undertaken, although they didn't have any further details. A dog unit appeared a short time later and the dog and handler probed the smoking debris. Looking for any signs of a survivor or human remains but found nothing. It was as though the arsonist had simply vanished as the CCTV cameras failed.

One thing though was for sure, this incident was going to take weeks of further investigation and reality suddenly hit Jack hard. The insurance would take months to sort out, even if they were to pay out against arson. There was now no building left to borrow against and the consortium were done for, as was Jack.

With only three days left to raise the rest of the money, he tried every means possible to raise it himself, but every avenue drew a blank. He couldn't even ask Lucifer to go in with him, as he'd also cut off all ties since being deceived at the auction. The day of completion was now upon him, as he headed to the auction house. Pleading with them for a couple more weeks or if they could give him his deposit back.

"Sorry Mr Skye… we sympathise with your plight obviously, but under the terms of the holding agreement you signed, you must complete on the sale within one calendar month. If completion stays unresolved after that point, then unfortunately the deposit is lost, and the lot is put up for resale."

He sat back in his Range Rover with his head on his steering wheel, bumping it up and down before slamming his hands down hard on the dashboard. The realisation of losing everything suddenly hitting and coming down hard on him. Staring out of his windscreen, he saw a figure walk out of the auction house. It was one of Lucifer's team from London, with a heap of documentation under their arm. His phone then pinged as a text message came in and he tapped the screen to open it. 'What was once yours is now mine, it's so easy to take from you, Jack, call it pay back, Lucifer.' He'd sent it from a withheld number so he couldn't reply.

Dejected and defeated, he slowly made his way home. Entering his flat an official looking letter sat on his door mat, he opened it to find it was from his mortgage lenders. He'd defaulted on three month's payments with no explanation given. Somehow his direct debit had failed and as a result they were beginning action to repossess. "Oh Shit," he shouted, he'd completely forgotten to make sure he'd left money in his account when he transferred it all ready for the auction deposit. Screwing the letter up he knew was stuffed, what could he do, where could he go, he had nothing left, he was bankrupt.

He took a bottle of brandy out of his drink's cabinet, poured a large glass and sank into his favourite chair broken and beaten. The only real thing he had left was Leila, but she too had turned her back on him. He downed the brandy and poured another as he stared at the wall in front of him. Running his fingers around the rim of the glass, he saw the old box on the side table. Safely nestled between his photographs and remembered the unread letter from his parents.

He grabbed the box flinging the lid across the room as he opened it and pulled out the envelope. Tossing the rest of the box behind him, where it hit the wall and split apart. Taking the letter out he opened the folded paper inside and slumped back into his chair. It was very short and almost written in a rush as he began to read.

Darling Jack our special boy,

Reading this means we are no longer with you and your grandparents are now also gone. You have probably worked out by now that things are not quite as normal as you thought and dark forces share and occupy our world. You have an important part to play in this and you have a requirement to fulfil that you were born into. The balance between good and evil is no longer aligned, and you must make this right.

The devil is at play and if successful will rule once more. You hold the key to prevent this from happening and we pray you can rise to the challenges that are to be asked of you.

You were born for a purpose and whatever life you have led to date, must now cease. You must become the man you are meant to be and destined for. Humanity is at risk; you must shoulder the responsibility and burden that will be placed on you.

Hopefully you are already in a safe place where dark forces cannot get to you and manipulate you. If you are not, then you are in grave danger and you must leave immediately. Head to the Mount, help will be waiting and there, all will be revealed.

Trust no-one and make your way there as quickly as possible.

All our love, mum, and dad.

He left his half empty glass and headed onto his balcony, looking to see if there was anyone around. It was late in the evening and at first, he could hear cats fighting. But then something else, strange sounds like hyenas laughing, as though something was hunting close by. He went inside closed the balcony doors and without further thought packed a rucksack. Knowing he wouldn't be returning, he put his door keys through the letter box, made his way down to his Range Rover and sped off into the night.

He had no idea where to go, only that the Mount must have meant Cornwall and tapped the previous destinations button on his route guidance. He drove through the night, feeling that he'd be safe and where all his questions would be answered. Arriving in Cornwall just before daybreak he decided to park up at Lizard point and watch the sun rise.

He sat on the bonnet with his back against the windscreen. Tucking his knees up under his chin, he wrapped his arms around them and wept as he rocked. Just as the sun started to peak above the ocean waves, he felt a sudden thought. His necklace started to glow and for the first time in ages, Leila was making contact. She was sharing thoughts of love again but not for him.

She was making love with Lucifer and was clearly enjoying herself. His subconscious mind must have somehow connected, as he could almost see them writhing below him, as if he was floating above looking down. Lucifer was on top of her and turned to look up. His face burned as though he'd been in a recent fire and his eyes were red like a demon's.

He looked pure evil and hissed as he spoke. "Hi, Jack, welcome to the fucking party. Once again what was once yours is now mine." Leila moaned and groaned in pleasure as she slid the fingers of her right-hand under her necklace and ripped it from her neck. The connection between them was instantly lost and he finally realised he'd lost her too. Showing no further emotion, he got back into his Range Rover and sped off heading for the Mount.

After making his way along the causeway and up onto a grassed slope, he sat on a bench. He was near the tree again where he'd spotted the familiar face previously and waited. It was still early, and the castle wasn't open yet, but he continued to patiently wait. Finally, after what felt like an age, a fully robed figure appeared and sat at the other end.

"A beautiful morning, don't you think?" came a voice from within the hood.

"I suppose so," replied Jack.

"You have a question brother?"

"Why am I her, why have I been drawn back here… to this place. Even when my worlds just fallen apart, I come here, why?'

"When I find myself lost, I like to go back to nature and look to the sky for some form of divine intervention. I find it tends to help." Removing the hood exposing his face in the process.

"You…you're the person I saw at the pond that day, feeding the ducks."

"Yes, Jack, I'm brother Peter."

"What's going on here… who am I really?"

"Come walk with me for a while and all will become clear."

They walked the grounds stopping every so often to take in the ocean's beauty and the gardens. The monk explained his sect were descendants of an ancient movement. Holy people known originally as the sect of Pictish Monks. Descendants of the Scottish Caledonii and other iron age tribes, where a small group broke away in late Roman times. Settling in the South before finally making their sanctuary in the mount itself. Burrowing deep into the rock, to make a large underground monastery below the castle.

He guided him inside the church and off to a side where an ancient looking door nestled and opened it. A small stone spiral staircase led down to the depths below. Dimly lit with old light fittings that pulsed and buzzed quietly as the power running through them fluctuated. At the bottom they came to another old oak door with a curved head, to which the monk pulled out a set of long rusty keys. Trying each one in turn mumbling to himself until he found the right one. Unlocking it he turned, smiled, and pushed it open to lead Jack through.

On the other side Jack stood mesmerised as a huge underground structure stretched out before him. Looking up into the roof, reminded him of being inside an old cathedral, both amazing and beautiful. He was led on where other monks started to appear, bowing their heads slightly as he walked past them. Although, he had no recollection, he felt he'd been there before. The other monks also seemed to know who he was as well.

They came to a large room stacked high with books. The old shelves almost groaning under the sheer weight as they ran around the entire room in a large curve. An old ladder on rollers giving access to any of the shelves in the room. The old stone floor heavily marked where the rollers had worn a groove into it over hundreds of years.

A table was set out in the middle of the room with a white cloth covering it and a double regal stand sat on top. The monk climbed the ladder and carefully looked before choosing a dusty old medieval book. He struggled to hold it under his spare arm as he climbed back down, due to its size and weight. "Now then," he said as he set it down on the table blowing the dust off.

"Sit down over there, Jack and let me explain what has brought you here and why you feel you've been here before." Jack took a seat and waited to be enlightened, he wasn't at all nervous he felt calm and safe instead.

"Prior to your parent's death, they asked us to keep an eye

on you and your brother. We watched you for years, keeping our distance, not interfering unless there was no other choice but to do so. You were watched all the time as you grew up, ensuring you were safe from evil. Making sure the devil couldn't get his hands on you, even when you got into drugs and into trouble. Your escapades to Amsterdam for example."

Staring at him disapprovingly before carrying on. "Then to the point where we lost you in France and you disappeared until reappearing a year later."

"When your friends were caught for drugs smuggling it was decided to fetch you in as you had become vulnerable. Tempted too far towards darkness and heading down a path that would lead to evil. The devil was now interested in you and thought you could be manipulated to take your brother's place. It even used its deadly sins to manipulate you in the process. But no-one thought you would take destiny into your own hands by leaving, even when Satan's followers were moving in on you. We kept them at bay until we lost you on that motorway in France but in doing so, we also knew Satan couldn't track you any longer either."

"You mean my whole life's been a farce —everything I've been through means nothing?"

"No not at all, Jack, you were born for something special, but your grandparents said you weren't ready. They wanted you to lead your own life until you were. Only now are you really ready for the burden that will shape your real destiny. A burden which you must shoulder and embrace from here on in."

Moving over to where the book was, he placed it on the regal stand, opening it on a specific section. "Religion comes in many strange forms and the story of Christ has also been told in many different forms over millennia. This ancient book tells of the story of the virgin birth and is a far cry from what religion and history has previously depicted."

He looked seriously at Jack, warning what he was about to be told would set out what lay ahead and began to read. "Leah was no virgin like the bible depicts. She was in sexual cahoots with a sorcerer who was said to have special powers. He was deformed and it is written that he was in fact half human, half beast."

"She became pregnant following their relations and cast aside by the towns people in disgust. A young man took pity on her, suggesting they pretend to be husband and wife and start afresh somewhere new as a family. They set off having no intention of stopping, unless for provisions when they needed to, but she soon tired and needed a rest. They stopped for a short while on the side of a dust track when a pony appeared in the gloom, willingly coming over when it saw them."

He turned the page and carried on.

"Leah was lifted onto its back, and they carried on. After some time, a snake laying coiled on the track, spooked the pony—it kicked out and bucked, throwing her to the ground where she lay holding her stomach in pain. The baby wasn't due, but the fall made it start to come early. She gave birth prematurely by the side of the track and the baby as a result was too weak and already dying. Matthew wrapped it in cloth and laid it by the side of the track. Putting stones around and over it to form a make-shift grave, knowing it had already died. He helped Leah back onto the pony advising they would have to stop in the next town to seek medical help, as she was still bleeding and weak."

Another page was turned.

"They could see a town lit up in the distance when she started to have pains again. Unknowingly, she had been carrying twins.

They found an old-disserted barn where she gave birth to a boy and spent the night there while she rested. Matthew keeping vigil to make sure she had no further serious complications. Despite being born premature as well, the boy survived and after a couple of days resting, they diverted to a town to get medical help. While there they registered themselves as a family, changing their names in the process.

"The sorcerer however started tracking them after finding out she was pregnant, and that they had left. Believing Leah belonged to him and no-one else, he wanted her back and the child for himself. He came across the stones and found the lifeless bundle. Angered that his child had been unceremoniously left, he used his dark powers to bring it back to life and in doing so, unknowingly created the devil in the process."

Jack stood up, "Lucifer?" the monk nodded.

"Yes… Satan… The Devil… Lucifer… The Anti-Christ… Diablo… they are all one and the same according to legend."

Peter then continued. "Jesus as he was named had no idea, he had a twin and grew up to be a kind, gentle man, inheriting his father's powers, which were used for good. For the devil however, this was a time of growing up unhappy, without a mother's love and guidance. Simply passed from one witch to another while the sorcerer moved around. Interested only in himself and partaking in his own ways, with no real time for the child. The devil felt unwanted and jealous of the other twin's success, became truly bitter and evil. Choosing the moment and time to take its revenge very carefully. Firstly, befriending and manipulating Pilot, just at the right time to help bring Christ's downfall."

Turning the page, he continued.

"Although the sorcerer had no time for the twins, he was

devasted to see his younger child crucified and wept for forgiveness as he slumped on the ground beneath the cross, staring up at him. Christ muttered something but by now was so weak, he couldn't be heard and died. Leaving the sorcerer mourning his dead son as he lay below him. Try as he may, his powers were not strong enough to bring him back, the devil had seen to that personally."

"The devil only saw weakness, in their father as he lay weeping for his dead son. Feeling betrayed, the devil challenged him, and they fought. However, the sorcerer couldn't be overpowered as they were too evenly matched. The devil therefore decided to strike an accord, agreeing not to battle further on one condition. This being every hundred years a young adult would be given to be its servant."

"To serve it, protect it and gather souls, which it would then be fed upon to keep it alive for all eternally. At the end of a hundred years' service, the servant would then be released. Transported back in time to when first taken to continue their lives as normal."

"Outraged by the demand, the sorcerer continued to battle but the devil had kept quiet about its real powers. It was far more superior and quickly weakened him. The sorcerer made a fist to protect himself, using his powers to whip lightning strands from his knuckles to keep the devil at bay. The Devil however drew a sword and with a swift blow, cut off his fist just below the wrist. Overwhelmed, the sorcerer fell to his knees begging for his life. In return the Devil agreed to spare his life, only if he would agree to its terms. Reluctantly he agreed and the devil produced a parchment and plucked a twig from the crown of thorns that had fallen from its dead brother's head. He dipped the end into Christ's blood, writing the terms of the agreement onto the parchment and forced him to sign it."

Another page was turned.

"The sorcerer signed then curled himself up the floor whimpering and broken. Picking up the fist by its wrist the devil started rotating it around its head. Beads of light started to form before making a whipping motion. Lightning threads tore from the knuckles, wrapping themselves around the sorcerer's body, squeezing and sucking the life out him. The devil stared on as the sorcerer looked back in terror, shaking violently as the strands sucked the soul clean from his body. He now lay lifeless, his face etched in fear as the devil claimed its first soul. Turning into a hideous beast, it kicked the body to one side vowing it was now the ruler of the underworld. Swearing it would wreak havoc on the earth itself. Not resting until the day, the gates to Tartarus could be opened to release the hounds of hell."

Peter closed the book and set it on the table as Jack processed the information before responding.

"I think I've seen this whip, in Lucifer's office wrapped in leather. He called it the Fist of God and explained in detail what it did. I asked if it worked but nothing happened when he tried?"

Jack then quickly came back to his original question, "What has all this got to do with me and my family why am I here?'

A voice came from the doorway as another older monk walked in. "Your family has everything to do with this, Jack, and you have been here before when you were very young." Peter bowed his head as the high priest walked in with another robed figure loitering slightly behind him.

"Come, my brother, come," beckoning the other figure in from outside the library. "Come in, there's no need to be afraid."

The figure entered the room and stood next to the table before speaking nervously.

"Last time I saw you… you were knee high to a grasshopper," as he dropped his hood to face Jack.

"John, is that you?"

"Yes… Jack it's me."

"But you're dead?"

"No… a simple story made up for Lucifer to think I was," as he ran over and hugged his younger brother tightly.

"Why John… why after all this time… where's mum and dad if you're alive?"

The high priest spoke again as the brothers parted. "There is much your brother needs to tell you my son, let the three of us walk and discuss."

As they slowly walked through the monastery, John filled Jack in on his story. "When I was twelve… I didn't become ill… I had a birth mark that started to change along with my moods as I began puberty. I was locked in my room for your own protection, our parents knew something paranormal was happening and they were concerned. Strange noises would be heard outside at night, like Hyenas communicating to each other. Trying to find a way in and on the odd occasion, a strange wiry figure would be seen staring up at me from the ground below."

"Our grandparents dabbled in the dark arts, they knew what was happening to me and placed a protection spell around the house so that evil couldn't enter. They were also aware of a cult that occupied the mount here and were able to make contact to see if they could help me."

"Help with what?" queried Jack as John pulled the hair up covering his left ear. The dark red markings of 666 could be clearly seen.

"It's the sign of the servant, I was born to serve the devil and our grandparents knew exactly what was going to happen, to me

174

and to you."

The high priest cut across and now spoke again. "My son, your brother is one of the unfortunate people. Chosen every hundred years to serve the Anti-Christ. Your parents told everyone that he had some infectious disease and had to be sent away for specialist treatment. Instead, he was brought here, where he could be protected. Learn our ways and understand how to defeat the devil and break the curse. Your parents stayed here too while you lived with your grandparents, occasionally returning home to visit you."

"You were brought here once, by your grandparents, to see your brother. It was a fleeting visit in the early hours one morning and you were tired being so young. Hence why you know this place but do not remember why. Lucifer eventually learned that your brother was here but had no way of accessing the monastery to get to him."

"Is this the Cornish myth about the pasties or has a spell been placed around it?" asked Jack, making the priest laugh.

"No... my son, the devil has simply never been invited."

"One night, your parents were on their way home to visit you, but he was waiting. As they turned a bend, he was in the middle of the road in the form of a hideous beast... holding his Fist of God as you call it... whipping lightning threads from it as they tried to swerve. Slicing through the car and making them lose control. They flew off the road smashing into a tree killing them on impact." Jack lowered his head not realising what they'd sacrificed trying to keep them both safe.

"Before they died, they asked us to keep John safe here. So, he couldn't be flushed out by the devil to become its servant. As part of this ruse, we made sure Lucifer's followers thought he'd died shortly after your parents. We were also asked to keep a watchful eye on you as well, to ensure Lucifer couldn't get near, which worked for a while."

"What happened then?" questioned Jack.

"You began mixing with the wrong people and Lucifer could see potential in you becoming his new servant instead of your brother. He had you followed everywhere you went, trying to get inside your mind to manipulate you. Remember the drugs, my son, the visions in the mirrors, this was not your mind playing tricks on you. You had found a way to unlock your mind and open a previously unknown gateway. Taking you straight to your brother's chambers and Lucifer found out about it. The only way John could keep himself safe was to throw holy water at it and shut it down every time it appeared."

"You must have always known subconsciously you're special, just like your brother here. Every hundred years when a child is born to be the devil's servant, so comes a further curse from the sorcerer as he died. As his soul was being sucked from his body, he managed to action one final act. The Devil Hunter... for every child born to serve the devil, so the next sibling will be born to kill it... in this instance that is you, my son."

"Why do think my grandparents had me change my name after they died then if they knew all this and how did they really die?"

"You were in terrible danger, Jack. When we notified them, we were coming to collect and train you... you disappeared... they knew the devil would force them to tell of your whereabouts so gave you strict instruction not to tell them. Lucifer appeared in their room one night, to force them to tell where you were, but they simply didn't know."

"Unfortunately... they fell victim to his whip, their souls ripped from their bodies as they lay in bed. The look of terror left etched on their faces, they sacrificed themselves for both of you and now you are here, finally together again. Your parents wanted you to change your name to help put him off your trail. When you re-appeared, you did as you were asked, but his sources were somehow made aware as well. He had the upper hand again and tried to manipulate you once more… when this failed… he took everything you had. Thinking he could then own you, but you escaped and now you are safe."

"Your training is starting very late; we should have collected you much earlier. Way before you disappeared, but nobody could foresee that you would tread your own path. Your grandparents were right to let you grow into a man before burdening you with your curse. I saw you had become a successful businessman that is a credit. It is a shame you fell afoul of the devil's trickery… you lost everything in the process… It is time to break the curse that envelops you and your brother, it is time to face your real destiny."

He looked to the other monks that amassed outside the library. Walking around them raising his arms as he spoke. "Time is quickly running out my brothers, soon the planets will start their alignment. Every thousand years the planets align, and evil will once more be able to rise from the depths of hell to walk upon the earth. The burden we must place on you, hunter is to break the curse and save humankind… you must kill the devil, you are the devil hunter."

Chapter 14

New Beginnings, New Ways

It had been six months since Jack had left his flat and turned his back on his old life for ever. Normal life had been replaced for a much simpler lifestyle. No fashion branded clothing, just white linen gathered in tightly like Buddhist's wear. He'd been training hard in the use and art of ancient weaponry that a devil hunter used. Spending many hours understanding and learning the history and requirements of the role he now embraced.

Early mornings were spent in deep meditation and contemplation, where he would sit facing towards a room named the Golden Chamber. As the devil hunter, he wasn't permitted inside without being in the presence of or being invited by the high priest himself and only then when the sign for his calling was coming. Breakfast consisted of a strict regime of fresh fruits, crusted breads, water, milk, or orange juice; sitting to eat in a large dormitory with the other monks. Long ancient benches and tables forming three lines in the room where they'd sit and eat in silence.

Following breakfast, his brother John would begin the days' training. Firstly, Capoeira or yoga in a hidden grassed area, where sea spray would lash up from the rocks below. Hitting them hard as they held their tight forms before finishing and moving to the main training arena. Despite the daily visitors to the Mount above, sightseers had no idea what lay beneath their feet. The area was cut into the rock face well away from view and the noise from the ocean masked any sounds made from below.

The weaponry was far from modern or superior, instead ancient and crude but effective. Stick fighting was fast, furious, and athletic. With the beatings being brutal when wrong moves were made, in a bid to make him learn quicker. Large heavy swords were also used, designed to quickly sap his strength but also to help build muscle, strength, and stamina. Along with shield and knife fighting, to train in close hand to hand combat. His favourite though, was archery, not with long bows but crossbows. His skill at hitting targets from both close and long range with pin-point accuracy made him a natural.

Following lunch, he'd head to the armoury where his brother would help him understand the weapons they had. Running through their history and capabilities. Each having its own story from the previous hunters that once owned them. He'd then spend the early afternoons testing them out on the shooting range, honing his skills as he tried to find one that suited him best. One item however was never discussed. Stored high up on a shelf wrapped in cloth. Jack had been through every weapon in the armoury except this one. He wanted to see what it was, but his brother always told him he wasn't ready.

Late afternoons were spent in the library reading and learning more about the dark arts. Plus, learning about the monks, themselves, where they originated and their different roles. Except the portal guardians, who he was never allowed to mix with or learn about. They were under the control of the high priest himself. He undertook their training and teaching regimes, away from the other monks and locked inside the Golden Chamber. All he knew was that their main purpose was to protect the chamber and were the ones that had helped keep track of him when he was growing up.

In the evenings he'd be summoned by the high priest where the pair would walk around the monastery. Listening to his teachings before heading up to the outside to observe the stars and planets. Sitting outside for hours where the high priest would talk about the importance of the heavens, the significance of the planets and their position in the universe. He always carried a brass rectangular box for their star gazing. After pin-pointing certain stars he'd turn it around showing its face. The cosmos and five planets were mapped out on its front and by turning a dial, he'd set the movement running.

He explained it was a two-thousand-year-old relic from Greece, named the Antikythera Mechanism. It was the only one two made, the other being found in a Roman shipwreck off Greece in 1901. It was so badly corroded however that scientists were unable to understand how it really worked. They thought the hand-powered device would have been used to predict eclipses and other astronomical events, but this wasn't its fully intended purpose.

By adjusting the dial to key astronomical points in the night sky, it would start to run and could predict the next alignment of the five planets on its face. The outer dial had notches cut in, each one having its own colour, Green, Amber, and Red. As the dial turned, one of the notches dropped into the next cog underneath, thus starting that one to turn to the next dial and so on, until all the notches and colours were engaged. If all were green, there was no risk, if amber the planets were due to start their alignment and if red, they were aligning.

Jack had noticed over the last month that the sequences had started to change from green to amber and now starting to change to red on some of the inner dials.

"You have a question to ask my son?" queried the high priest.

"I've seen the inner dials change from green to amber and now they're starting to turn red, meaning the planets are starting to align... what does that mean for us?"

"Change is coming, feel the cold wind coming in off the ocean. It is early summer, yet the night air is cold, evil is starting to rise once more, we have little time left. Remember the land you purchased for Lucifer and the warehouses you lost to him. They have a connecting significance to the planet's alignment, do you know what this is?"

"Yes master... Leila had told me about their significance, but I didn't believe her at the time. She studied the history and importance from her research archives. The three land parcels are connected by ley lines and form a triangle, which have a powerful energy force running through them. The warehouses are at their epicentre where sacrifices used to take place. She said if they were reconnected, a portal to the lower realm could be opened and evil would rise once more. But that can never happen as the ley lines were cut following a battle between good and evil and the devil was forced to flee."

He then continued.

"According to her archives, after the devil fled the battle, the guardians had deep trenches dug. Severing the lines and cutting off the powerful forces that ran through them. The trenches were filled and lined with lead so they couldn't be reconnected. But now Lucifer has full control of them, he'll be able to reconnect them again."

"It was a great battle," the high priest replied. "The devil hunter aided by the portal guardians had the devil trapped but it had anticipated this. Throwing its servant, the hunter's brother between them for protection. Leaving him with no choice but to kill him, giving the devil the chance to escape."

"That's terrible... why do that... there was no need to kill him?"

The high priest turned to him and spoke more seriously. "His brother was born to be the devil's servant that was his curse, as the devil hunter he was also cursed just as you are. The hunter knew his brother had turned evil and in doing so, his main objective was to protect his master. It was a case of kill or be killed. Your brother's curse is also to serve the devil and if placed in his clutches, he will turn. He will gather souls for his master, and he will protect him."

"For you as the hunter, your brother, when turned will try and kill you. Most hunters have fallen foul of this and over millennia, murdered by the servant before they could get to the devil. When the time comes you will face the same choice, kill John before he kills you. The only way to save you both is by destroying the devil to break the curse. All previous hunters knew this. This hunter had no choice but to kill his own brother to try to get to the devil."

"What happened to him after he killed his brother?"

"He died... once he'd killed his brother, he failed to exist anymore as he hadn't killed the devil to release them both. A hundred years later and a new servant was born, along with a new hunter and so the cycle has continued right up to now. Previous hunters have either faced the same fate or the devil has killed them before the servant was killed. The only changes this time are we have your brother here, where the devil cannot reach him. But the pull to serve is getting stronger, eventually we will be unable to keep him safe any longer. He will seek out the devil himself and will turn."

"I can't kill my own brother... I... I... it's not possible... it's not in me to do it." He dropped his head in disgrace and pulled his knees in tight where he sat wrapping his arms around them like a child. The high priest put a hand on his shoulder to comfort him.

"My son, your destiny is laid out in front of you, a path that only you can follow. To save you both you must destroy Satan or be destroyed in the process. If your brother turns evil and presents himself to you, he will most certainly try to kill you or take your soul to feed to his master. Either way you would be doomed, it is therefore better to die freeing him of his own curse, by sacrificing yourself in the process, unless you kill the devil and free the both of you."

He looked at the Antikythera Mechanism and ran his finger along the notches. "Soon the sign will be here, and you must take up arms as the hunter." He turned the box around and the planets had started to slowly move across its face.

"Once they align the portal will open and evil will rise once more to take control of the upper realm. You are our only remaining hope and chance to stop this."

He slept uneasily that night, pondering when his brother would eventually turn and whether he could save him before it happened. He fell asleep assuring himself to demand seeing the wrapped weapon, high up on the shelf in the armoury during his next training session.

The next day's routine was just the same as any other up until lunch as Jack was feeling uneasy. Knowing his older brother was a ticking time bomb and he may have to kill him. He headed over to the armoury as soon as he'd finished to confront him.

"I take it from your speed to get here and silence on arrival, you know what my curse brings for us both?" Jack just nodded and pointed to the shelf above. John didn't hesitate and nodded back in agreement; it was time for him to see what it was. Putting a ladder against the shelving, John climbed up and fetched the wrapped parcel down.

Jack was already sat on the floor in a half lotus position. Waiting just as he had done so with all the previous items he practiced with. He carefully unfolded the cloth to reveal its contents, with John then telling the history of it.

"This crossbow was last used in 1631, during the witch trials of Wurzburg in Germany. The devil had been trapped within a group of one hundred and fifty-seven men, women, and children. All deemed to be the devil's worshippers. They couldn't identify which one was the devil despite calling out for it to show itself. The towns folk therefore took to burning and beheading the crowd, one by one to force the devil out of the pack."

Sitting himself down, John continued as he drew a picture of the scene in the dust on the floor. "The devil was cornered and transformed itself into a hideous beast. Killing people in waves as it swung and lunged around in a bid to escape. The devil hunter was already there and waiting of course. This crossbow belonged to that hunter, his name Johnsen Himmel. It's only been fired twice, both times attempting to kill the beast with a hit direct to its heart."

"His first shot used a standard crossbow bolt, hitting the beast clean in the chest but had no effect. The Devil simply pulled it straight out. The hunter reached back into his pocket and pulled out a slightly longer nail, with a slight curve to it and fired again. The nail struck the beast to its left shoulder, causing it to weaken and transform back to its human form. However, as he moved in for the kill, he was distracted, and the devil killed him."

Picking the two nails up from the cloth he continued,

"The two nails here are part of a group of three. The third being lost when it was fired in 1631 when the devil hunter died. It's thought to be still embedded in the devil's shoulder to this day. These nails are extremely important and toxic to the devil, the only known thing that will destroy it with a hit directly to its heart."

"What's so special about them?" Jack asked.

"The three nails were used to nail Christ to his cross when he was crucified. They're slightly misshapen due to hitting bone as they were hammered in. This was done so that none of his followers could try to cut him down and rescue him. The devil plotted Christ's downfall and ensured the Romans took this action instead of tying him in place. In doing so, the nails became saturated with Christ's blood and are poisonous to the devil as a result. One twins blood used to kill the other."

Jack nestled the butt of the crossbow into his shoulder, bringing his other forearm up to support it. Using his other hand, he put his index finger on the trigger. "Jack, you're the first devil hunter since Johnsen Himmel, who's been able to shoulder the weapon perfectly.

The crossbow was made to fit his measurements and size exactly. You must have the same measurements; this is a good omen." Jack turned the bow towards his brother, eyeing him through the cross hairs and a click was heard. John looked startled, without realising it, Jack had squeezed the trigger and was pointing it straight at his brother's heart.

"Sorry," he said, "I got a little carried away, it sort of felt like instinct. It's a good job it wasn't loaded, and the string pulled back."

"When the time comes, my brother, you will have to do what is required as the hunter. I fully understand that," pulling his hair up from the back of his ear to show his sign again. "It's becoming more raised; the planets are starting to align. Soon you'll be called to arms, and you must be ready. Let's try this weapon out on the range, it looks perfect for you."

The weapon was in pristine condition just as the others were. Well cared for they and lovingly kept throughout the ages. They spent the rest of the afternoon firing bolts at different targets. Both moving and fixed, hitting them with pin-point accuracy from any angle and any distance, he was finally ready.

"There's nothing more I can train you with Jack, your skills are complete and the weapons perfect for you. There's no more I can teach you either, your lessons are in essence complete."

"I'll leave you to continue your own for a while. I must make my own preparations now for when your calling comes." John bowed to his brother, turned, and made his way back up the grassy slope between the rocks and towards the monastery. Sightseers visiting the mount above, still none the wiser of what was happening below them.

Jack turned to the ocean and saw the sun was slowly starting its decent. He sat facing it, feeling the warmth on his face as he went into a deep meditative state. The high priest stood on the rocks above looking down with his hands behind his back. Having watched him training with the crossbow, he nodded in agreement that he was ready and turned away. Heading straight to the Golden Chamber and closing the great doors behind him as he entered.

It was around midnight when Jack came out of his trance. The sound of the waves crashing below, bringing his senses back to life. He opened his eyes to see the high priest sitting opposite in a half lotus position. His eyes closed deep in meditation, like he'd been meditating with him. He moved his legs to get the circulation moving again, but as he did, the high priest open an eye, just for the slightest of moments.

He put his hands down to start to push himself up when he heard a whoosh. The high priest had a large stick by his side and pounced, swinging the stick towards his head. There was a loud bang as the stick was stopped in mid-blow by Jack's. He'd kept his own weapon behind him and reacted with lightning speed.

The stick fight was fast and furious, the high priest hitting him with everything he had. Jack was forced back towards the main training area in defence. In the bushes around him he could here rustling and saw shadows quickly moving about, then sounds like hyenas communicating. The high priest had the look of evil about him as he attacked again. This time even harder, before more figures appeared, putting even more pressure on Jack's defence.

Using his skills, he quickly took two of them down, before taking out a third and badly injuring a fourth. When the fighting abruptly stopped, and the remaining figures moved apart. Leaving him facing the high priest who now had his back to him. He made ready for further battle as he slowly turned dropping his hood. Instead of the high priest, Lucifer was now staring back. Tilting his head from side to side then wiping his mouth across a sleeve of his robe. Jack swung straight into action with his fighting stick; Lucifer then beating him back with ease and with a fast strike, snapped Jack's clean in half.

He quickly moved backwards in panic until he fell against one of the targets and tumbled over. Lucifer now standing above him had his fist of God ready. Swinging it around his head as small beads of blue light started to form. Slowly growing into lightning strands the longer they stretched. With a final whip back, the strands shot forwards, tightening around him as they hit. He could feel them pulling at his very soul and was panic stricken. Terrified by what was happening and unable to move everything went black.

Slowly opened his eyes again, he was surrounded by portal guardians with the high priest cradling him.

"Your training is indeed complete, but you cannot control your nerves. You fear the devil and it will therefore easily destroy you."

Jack looked back at him. "But you were Lucifer, master, you attacked me. I couldn't defend myself; I wasn't ready, I didn't have the weapon."

"He was not here at all, my son, I tapped into your mind's eye while you were deep in meditation. I could see the struggle and torment you are having. You cannot control your feelings your emotions are controlling you. You are unsure of how your family and old friend Reg really died. What you just experienced is what they would have felt, but simple toys and distractions were used in instead."

"The whip here, a simple fairground toy that shoots out flecks of light along thin strands of plastic. The shadows, and animal noises, were not demons at all. The guardians were role playing but the noises are what you will experience when you face the devil for real. Lucifer was just me, play acting his mannerisms and the rest was already in your mind."

"The lightening and tightness around your body, a simply modified taser. Enhanced to make you feel like your soul was being sucked out. Its high voltage knocked you unconscious, but it was designed to feel very real."

"We only have days left before you're calling, and you are still scared. The Devil has taken everything you had, wealth... happiness... friends... family... Leila. The Devil must die to allow the second coming to happen."

"Christ needs to rise again and take back control, Good must prevail over evil. Currently evil has the upper hand, to complete the final test, you must learn to control your nerves. Come, my son, we will study and meditate together. Tonight's failure still leaves much to prepare for and to discuss." He was helped up off the ground and led away. The high priest supporting his beaten body.

The pair headed to the priest's main chambers where the large old oak door was banged shut behind them and bolted from the inside. They mediated and talked for two long days, the high priest sharing his own knowledge of the dark arts and other secrets. Secrets that had only ever been shared with other devil hunters through the ages. John wandered the monastery's vast rooms aimlessly during this time. Concerned his brother would crumble and fail at the final test. However, as the third day began, the noise of a bolt being released was heard. Echoing through the silent corridors as the high priest's chambers were unlocked.

He ran to the chambers where the high priest was stood outside with the door open. Inside Jack was sitting deep in mediation with a glow around him. He'd finally mastered control of his feelings and was ready. His necklace had been repurposed since its twin had been lost. It now served as a mechanism to hide his emotions from being felt by others as well as help heal. The high priest advised that the necklaces power had weakened somewhat but it would protect him. So long as the devil didn't try to manipulate his weaknesses.

From the echoes, a voice began shouting out, summoning the high priest to the Golden Chamber. The statue had started to cry tears and the cauldron had begun to fill. He quickly made his way there, shutting the large double doors behind him as he entered. A short time later the soft ring of a bell was heard, and the Chambers Guardians hurried past to join him inside.

It was early the next day when he finally reappeared at his personal chambers again. Jack remained in his meditative state and John was watching over him He put a hand on John's shoulder and lifted the hair up from behind his left ear. The devil's mark was far more prominent and darker in colour, it was time.

Clapping his hands, Jack opened his eyes and looked over at the high priest. "Is it time for my calling master?"

"Yes, my son… walk with me to the library, there are things to run through before we head to the Golden Chamber. Tomorrow at sundown you will receive the sign, calling you to arms. In the meantime, we must complete our final preparations in the Chamber itself."

The pair walked through the corridors towards the library, the high priest with his hands behind his back seemingly pondering. "When we finish here today, you will leave and head to the edge of the ocean and wait. Tomorrow you will receive the sign to take up arms, hunter. From there head to the warehouses where the devil will be preparing to open its portal. There you will face the beast and kill it, finishing its reign on this earth."

The pair entered the library for a final teaching session as the high priest read from the Garima Gospels on the deadly sins. From there they headed to the armoury to collect the crossbow and moved onto the Golden Chamber, where they entered. The monks were congregated in a mix of prayer and meditation as younger monks continued further preparations. Every time one process was completed then the same process would be repeated.

Under Christ's statue a large black cauldron was slowly filling. Droplets of water coming from its eyes that ran down its body to feed into a trough, which then led into a cauldron. The high priest now turned to face Jack directly. "For now, I can share no more with you my son, it is time for you to leave this place."

Gathering the crossbow and nails, Jack was led back to the chambers main doors and shown out. Leaving the monks to continue their own preparations alone. Tucking the leather goat's skin under his arm, he made his way back through the monastery towards the ancient winding staircase. From there he made his way up to the church above and waited at the back for the public to leave. As the last of them left, he started making his way through the mount's main public areas and down to the causeway.

Stopping midway he looked back to see the high priest watching. He nodded respectfully, placed his hands behind his back and turned to head back towards the church. Jack carried on across the causeway back to the mainland and headed off to where his Range Rover was stored.

On the beach Jack sat waiting for the sign not really knowing what to expect as the sun began to slowly sink. He stood up and impatiently stared out at the ocean as it began kissing the top of the water. 'It's not going to happen, the high priest got it wrong,' he thought to himself in frustration. Yet as it disappeared below the water line, a bright blue flash occurred, spreading quickly landwards towards him.

Just as it hit, a strong gust of wind pushed him slightly off balance bathing him in blue light. Holding his arms out to help balance himself, his hair and clothes rustled violently before it disappeared. The sign had come, and he knew it was time to take up arms.

Making his way back up the beach, he headed to the car park to his Range Rover and got in. Sitting for a short while, he reflected on the life he used to have as he gripped the steering wheel. Then touching his necklace, he asked it to heal him if he were to become injured and started the engine. With one last look in his wing mirror, he drove off into the early evening heading for the warehouses where his destiny awaited.

Turning into the alleyway at the warehouse's, a white limousine slowed. Flashing its lights into the darkness to signal its arrival, before slowly moving forwards again. As it drew level with one of the buildings, a robed figure appeared from the shadows. Trying to see into the back through a half open rear window, before sinking back. A pair of red eyes then stared at him from inside as it drove past, and the window shut again.

A curtain of pure energy parted like waves as it slowly drove through into the darkness beyond. The figure then reappeared, trying to follow before it resealed, only to be bounced off as he reached it. Putting his hands on the energy force, he pushed hard. Managing to push it inwards, only for it to deflect again, as if he were pushing against a bubble that wouldn't burst.

Demons guarding the other side hissed and spat at him as he tried to break through. "You do not pass this way today," they mocked, "your time will come." Prodding at the wall of energy with their prongs warning him off. Accepting defeat, he retreated to the safety of the streetlights and lowered his hood. Reaching into his robes he pulled out a cell phone and pushed the button to call the pre-programmed number.

A car radio was suddenly interrupted as a cell phone sprung into life, vibrating in the cup holder of the arm rest. Pushing the call accept button on the console, a voice came through the car's speakers.

"He has arrived my brother."

"Is she with him?"

"I am unsure, the windows of the limousine were blacked

192

out with only a rear one slightly open. I could see someone else in the back with him, but I couldn't tell if it was her, I'm not totally sure sorry."

There was silence for a few seconds, as Jack contemplated the situation and sighed deeply. After all they'd been through, he still couldn't believe she'd given in to temptation and betrayed him. "Okay, John, thanks for the update, I'll be there soon. I'm about an hour away, is the keeper with you?"

"Yes, my brother."

Ending the call, the radio burst back into life and Jack started to reminisce about his lost love. The fun and happiness they'd shared together prior to the devil seducing her. Happy thoughts then turning to resentment, then anger. Realising she was now in the hands of the man who'd destroyed everything he had. He calmed his feelings, burying them deep as he gripped his necklace. Its energy glowing to help hide his emotions before turning the radio up to take his mind off things.

Pulling into a space near the alley, he was met by the monk as he opened his boot to take out the wrapped antiquities.

"I'm sorry I couldn't tell you before brother, but I'm the keeper. I couldn't allow you to know this as it would have interfered with our learning and training sessions."

Taken aback slightly Jack responded. "It's fine, John, don't worry about it, nothing surprises me anymore. As the keeper, the high priest advised you'll have some additional weaponry for me that wasn't at the monastery?"

"Yes," pulling a sack from behind a set of waste bins. He started to rummage inside, pulling out an old battered long leather coat and leather brimmed hat. Jack then questioning what he could possibly do with them.

"This coat and hat will protect you from the acid in the

demon's spittle. If you go into the realm unprotected their acid will kill you within a matter of seconds."

Next came a belt with five vials attached. "Holy water from the tears of Christ," the monk explained. "When you get to the end of the alley, throw one of these at the floor and a wall of water will appear. It will keep the demons at bay long enough for you to take your shot."

"What's the others for?" he said, holding one in his hand to feel how it fitted.

"The only way to get out once you're in the devil's realm is to open a portal. The Devil was cursed by Christ as he died and as such has a weakness. When the devil is vulnerable eight red doors appear. Portal doorways allowing the devil hunter every chance possible to escape without being destroyed."

"To open one, you must throw a vial of holy water at it. Christ's tears will change the door from red to black opening a portal back to the Golden Chamber. The chamber is the key you see. When you activate a portal door, it turns from black to red in the chamber and opens, the guardians are then able to assist in helping you back through."

"If you fail however, they'll use the portal to recover the antiquities before they can fall into the hands of evil. You must be aware though brother, once you activate one you will only have a few minutes before it closes again. If one closes so you must open another and the guardians will try and assist again."

Chapter 15

12 July 2020 - Re-awakening

"Can you hear me… open your eyes… he's still breathing but not really conscious." The medics equipment bleeping loudly as they worked hard trying to save him. One of them stood up to ask questions of the small crowd that had gathered, while the other continued to try and stabilise his life signs.

"Does anyone know what happened here? Does anyone know who this is?"

"Yes," said a voice as john stepped forwards.

"He's my brother, this is Jack… Jack Skye."

"His heartbeat's erratic—he's going into arrest," shouted the other medic from the ground. Quick get the pads on while I try and stem the bleed from his head."

"Okay charging… clear," thump.

"Again… charging… clear," thump.

"It's no good we're losing him, charge again to 200."

"Charging… clear," thump. "It's no good."

"Come on, Jack, don't do this… hang in there, buddy, come on… charge again."

"Charging… clear," thump. His body jolted again but was lifeless.

A hazy glow was all that Jack could now see, the voices in the background became quieter and more slurred. He felt himself slipping, slowly drifting further and further away. Voices becoming dimmer, slower, as his thoughts started to wander.

"Can you hearrrrrr meeeeeeee." His mind now travelling back to his past as he his necklace tried its hardest to heal him, bleep, bleep, bleeeeep, bleeeeeeeeeeeeeep, bleeeeeeeeee, drifting, drifting until silence.

There was a loud banging noise as the paramedics crashed his trolley through the A&E Dept doors where a team of doctors were waiting. "This is Jack Skye, a thirty-three-year-old with gun shots to his arms, legs, and a shot to the head. We've given him adrenalin and managed to restart his heart. His pulse is very weak his blood pressure's low... he's arrested twice on-route and we've managed to bring him back each time. It's over to you guys now... good luck."

The crash team took control as one of the doctors stood over the trolley, taking over with the breathing mask. Pumping it every few seconds to keep the air going in. Jack's eyes were barely open, flickering as he fell in and out of consciousness. Lights flashing above him as they sped their way along the hospital's corridors.

"We're losing him again," voices becoming softer and softer as his vision blurred and he drifted heading towards the small light in the distance. "Okay with the paddles... stand clear everyone," thump.

"Go again...charging... clear," thump.

"Let the surgeons know we're coming in hot... go again... charging... clear,' thump. The doors slammed open as the trolley was rushed into the operating theatre, where the surgeons stood anxiously waiting for his arrival.

Eight hours later the lead surgeon found John sitting in the prayer room alone. Staring at the different colours shining through the stained-glass window, set above Christ's statue on a crucifix. As the light shone through, Christ's image appeared to smile slightly. The surgeon stood next to him with his hands together, resting on his stomach.

"Mr Johnson, isn't it?"

"Brother John thanks," he smiled back. "Do you have news on my brother... did he survive?"

"I must say I have never come across anyone that has been so keen to cling to life. It's been a difficult a few hours and we almost lost him a few times, but somehow we kept pulling him back. The wounds to his arms and legs were easy to treat and these injuries should make a full recovery... but his head wound was more complicated... A neurologist had to be called to deal with the wound to his head. Luckily the bullet was removed along with the majority of shattered skull fragments lodged in the left side of his brain, he was very lucky; the bullet was made of silver and caused less damage. A normal bullet would have killed him instantly at such a close range."

"Thank you, doctor, what happens now?"

"Well... he'll need to stay here for a few weeks at least. Currently have him in a controlled coma to allow time for his head injury to heal. So until he regains consciousness we won't really know if he has sustained any major brain injuries or not, only time will tell. In the meantime we'll monitor his condition while the brain swelling eases and then replace the piece of skull that had to cut away."

John looked concerned. "Don't worry he's in good hands here, brother John. Do you have a number we can contact you on to keep you updated?"

"Erm... yes I have this one," pulling a phone out of his robe pocket. "Can you get the number out of it, I'm not so good with technology?"

"Yeah, sure let me help you... oh and I almost forgot... if you report to reception, they have his personal things waiting for you to collect."

The surgeon took the number and went to leave as he handed it back, only to stop and turn again. "Erm... brother John, there was a necklace around your brother's neck. It was the strangest thing and no-one else seemed to see it... but... I couldn't help but notice a faint glow coming from it. As it got dimmer, he seemed to become more stabilised, until it faded away completely. After that we had no more issues with his vital signs?" He scratched his head as he walked away talking to himself, "The strangest of things, weird."

John decided to head back to the mount and await news there. The longer he was away from the monks, the more at risk he was of being found by the devil and turning. If he transformed now, Jack would be at serious risk of him killing him. He was glad to be met outside by some smartly dressed individuals. Guardians who were sent by the high priest to help escort him safely back to the mount.

Daily messages were received on his progress but despite the wounds healing, there was no improvement from Jack himself. He was still in a coma but the swelling on his brain had reduced enough for them to repair the section of missing skull. The doctors couldn't fully explain what was happening as he should have regained consciousness by now. So, they advised he may never regain consciousness, due to the level of injury his brain must have sustained.

The high priest sat in his chambers pondering. If Jack never recovered, brother John would soon turn and become the devil's servant. For at least the next hundred years he would do the devils bidding. Nothing could prevent it and it meant hundreds and hundreds of souls would be lost. Far worse, nothing now could prevent the portal to the gates of hell from being opened either. Without a devil hunter, all was lost.

Three weeks had now past since his skull reconstruction and there were still no signs of improvement. The doctors continued their daily checks, flicking their torch pens into his eyes, looking for the slightest response but nothing. The high priest walked the corridors, contemplating whether the necklace had fully worked. Yes, it had saved his life, but did it have enough energy reserve to complete the healing process before its power was finally spent?

Using it to help hide his nerves from the devil may have been a push too far for it. He decided to try and make a kinetic connection with Jacks mind. Drawing a seven-sided star on the floor, he finished by making a circle in the middle of it. Before sitting inside, he drew letters in each of the segments, spelling the word sanctum and dropped in some runes with letters on. He then sat in the circle and set his mind into a deep trance as he meditated.

He found himself in a strange tranquil sort of place, walking along a beach. Waves gently washing along the soft golden sands, and he found the sound calming and soothing. Ahead sitting in silence ahead was someone soaking in the sun's rays. Their arms wrapped around their legs, as they looked out towards the ocean, breathing in the fresh sea air. The beach was completely empty as he looked around, and apart from the gentle sloshing of the waves there was silence.

He could tell it was Jack, sitting back from the water's edge, seemingly in a contemplative mood. Picking up a handful of sand and watching the tiny grains gently fall slowly through his fingers. The high priest continued to watch as a group appeared, slowly making their way down towards the water's edge. Reaching where he was sitting, they sat in a line next to him, staring at him. The high priest now took his turn, choosing to sit facing them with his back to the sun and the water. Jack however didn't react, instead engrossed with the sound of the ocean and the smell of the fresh sea air. Appearing to have no recognition of his surroundings nor the people next to him.

At the top of the cliffs nearby he noticed Leila viewing them from above, smiling down at him. Happy he was alive but when beckoned, she turned and walked away. The high priest knew her full memory couldn't join them. She'd become an advocate of the devil and her soul doomed to walk in loneliness forever after he killed her. Trapped with no way of finding the light that would lead her to the heavens above. All Jack would have left were what memories remained in his head.

The priest looked at the others and knew their faces all too well. They'd been created by Jack's subconscious mind, probably at the point when the necklaces energy was spent, leaving the healing process not fully completed. His body and soul had somehow become disconnected, and he appeared to be stuck in a boyish state, waiting to be told what to do. The high priest held his hands upwards and began to speak.

"Jack, around you are the memories of the people you have a deep love for. Your parents here wish to return to your mind and body if you will let them, signalling for them come across. "Richard… Elizabeth please join by my side here." They stood up and took their place beside him. He moved his gaze to the next couple. "Jack these are the memories of your grandparents, and they too wish to return to your mind and body if you will let them. "James… Silvia please come and join on the other side of me." He then moved his gaze once more to an older gentleman. "Jack this is the memory of Reg, one of your longest and dearest friends. He wishes to return to your mind and body if you will let him. Reg come and join behind me if you please." He then beckoned Jack to rise.

he stood up and walked forwards stopping just in front of him. "Remember our time together and my teachings in the dark arts. We talked about what could happen if you became trapped and unable to escape. You instructed the necklace to save you, but its energy was spent before it could fully complete its work. Some of your key thoughts memories are missing as a result." He moved sideways and led Jack to the water's edge where the waves lapped over his feet. He curled his toes feeling the warm water and the soft sand squidging between them.

"Richard… Elizabeth if you please," guiding them towards Jack, where they walked into his body from behind. "James… Silvia if you please," and guided them towards Jack where they also walked into his body from behind. "Finally, you Reg, if you please," guiding him in the same manor until he entered Jack's body. "Now for Jack, come sit with me at the water's edge," and as Jack sat, his eyes started to glow a bright bluey white as though an energy force was building inside him.

The high priest spoke again, "An old friend once spoke some wise words to me as I pondered on a problem." Staring into his eyes as he continued. "I tend to find myself drawn to nature when I'm trying to understand or deal with a problem. Sometimes you just need a little divine intervention and look up to the sky above." Jack showed signs he recognised this somewhere in his deepest thoughts, as he continued playing with the water and the wet sand.

He then gazed skywards remembering the parson on the bench feeding the ducks. The high priest now whispered in his ear. "Mind, body and soul together as one again." Touching his forehead with his fingers, then blew hard onto his face making him fall backwards onto the sand.

He jolted heavily taking a huge breath as though for the first time and sat bolt upright in his hospital bed. Pulling the tubes from his mouth and throat, coughing, and gagging heavily in the process. He then pulled out the drips and sensors that were attached to the machines monitoring him. He'd come out of his coma and was becoming alert as he looked around his surroundings.

Nurses hearing the alarms from the machines as he disconnected himself, burst in thinking it was an emergency. Only to be left baffled how he was suddenly awake. He could talk, he could use his hands and arms, he could move his legs and feet and when the bandages were removed from around his head, the wound had all but healed. His left eye however was now brown while his other remained blue.

A day later he was walking again, albeit shakily at first, then discharging himself three days later. The guardians then taking him back to the mount before the police could catch up asking questions about the shooting. He was still shaky on his legs as they arrived and had to be helped down to the monastery below. On arrival he was greeted by monks bowing their heads just as they'd done so when he very first arrived.

He was taken to his quarters to continue his rehabilitation and as he sat in his bed the high priest appeared. He thanked him for his help the priest nodding in return. Telling him to get some rest as his teachings and training would recommence as soon as possible. The crossbow and Christs remaining crucifix nail had been recovered so there was still hope the devil could be defeated but there was now another problem. The portal to the lower realm would also soon be opened, spies had advised the ley lines were nearly fully reconnected again.

After the high priest left, his brother knocked and entered holding a clear crystal. "Use this it has healing powers and will complete what your necklace was unable to. The high priest has summoned you to meet with him as soon as possible and continue your teaching in dark arts." He took the crystal and laid down holding it on his chest as John left, closing the door behind him.

The room became bathed in a white glow as the power in the crystal started to come alive. Flickering and pulsating, turning his hands into a bright white glow. It's healing powers slowly made their way up his arms and then into the rest of his body. As the glow reached his neck, he felt a slight tightness. All he could then see was white, as the healing powers fully engulfed him, making him fall asleep.

He slept solidly for twenty-four hours before waking and making his way to the large refectory for something to eat. As he entered there were whispers and as he sat, there were nods of heads as monks let each other know of his reawakening. He sat eating quietly before being joined by his brother. He stared admiringly at him, happy that he'd survived his bout with the devil and there was still a chance.

After the meal Jack made his way to the grass area overlooking the ocean to meet with the high priest. He could hear the waves crashing on the rocks below as he headed to his favourite spot. The high priest was already there meditating so he sat down next to him.

"You summoned me to meet you here master?" he said as the priest held up a finger. Gesturing for him to be quiet and listen to the noise of nature in full force. He could smell the fresh clean sea air and hear the waves crashing below, as the spray splashed up high, wetting their faces. "It makes you feel alive my son doesn't it, you can feel natures natural forces in action."

He turned to Jack observing he was well again apart from one of his eyes, which was now brown in colour. "It would seem the devil left its mark on you hunter. A trophy from your first encounter I see… but it will not be your last… take this crossbow and shoot from here, at the target that is lit up."

Jack nestled himself between the rocks, pulled the string back hard locking it into position and loaded bolt. Taking aim he fired, missing the target completely. "Try again," ordered the priest and he missed again. "Hmm… now move in closer and try again."

He moved further down the training area until he was about 20meters away from the target and knelt by the side of another. He loaded the crossbow again, took aim and fired. This time just hitting the edge, but nowhere near the target's inner rings or bullseye.

He moved closer again until he was around five meters away and loaded. This time standing to fire and hit the target in the bullseye. Tuning to face the high priest he was asked to re-join him on the rocks. "You're at a slight disadvantage now hunter, you will have to keep your brother near to be able to get close enough to the target, lets pray he doesn't turn before this happens. In the meantime, we must go to the Golden Chamber and review the planets alignment in more detail. We can then gauge when it will be the best time to attack again. I have asked your brother to join us there as well."

They met John at the large double doors of the chamber and the high priest knocked with the bottom of his staff. The doors creaked open to show the golden glow of the chamber and the black portal doors once more. The small group of guardians protecting the room bowed, then quickly left. The chamber itself looked as though nothing had ever happened in there. The cauldron beneath Christ's statue was empty and the compass in the floor was dull in colour. Light and shadows still bounced around the room from the large wax candles, as their flames flickered and danced.

The brothers were invited to sit and meditate while the high priest walked up the steps to fetch a large book from the alter. Returning to where they were, it covered his lap when he sat down and opened it. Flicking through the pages he found the ancient text he was looking for and clicked his fingers to bring the brothers out of their meditative states.

In the roof space above the same floating illusion of the cosmos was there. The planets slowly moving and spinning showing what was happening in the cosmos. Mercury, Venus, Mars, Jupiter, and Saturn; the five planets indicated on the face of the Antikythera Mechanism, were starting their final alignment phases. Jack knew the portal to the lower realm would soon be open and the beasts of hell would be released.

The high priest explained how the early solar system began, suffering very violent and turbulent beginnings. Huge energy forces were produced as planets spun and split away from their tight clusters. Some colliding and engulfing others to form larger planets while some spun off like billiard balls shooting out into the cosmos.

The gravitational forces of the new planets working against each other, ripping, and tearing themselves apart as they moved across the new solar system. Finding their final positions where in ancient Greek mythology, the gods lived. The violent negative forces and beginnings of dark matter then creating dark energy, making the newest planet forming vulnerable. It was already large when it was struck, spewing a third of its mass out into space. But it had enough positive energy within it to hold the mass within its own gravitational pull, forming a smaller satellite.

The earth and moon were then finally formed. Their positive forces allowing life to begin, with the moon in a synchronous rotation, moderating the planet's wobble. This then led to a relatively stable climate to be formed. The moon causing tides and creating a rhythm that has then guided humans ever since. As the solar system continued to create itself, so too other forces were created in the chaos, thus good and evil then came to be.

He then read from another passage in the ancient Greek book where a prediction had been made in the sixth century by Pherecydes of Syros which he translated.

"Before the earth was in order a cosmic battle ensued, Cronus the head of one side -representing evil and Ophioneus the leader of the other representing good. Ophioneus and his brood ruled over the early cosmos and with it, good settled its previous dark chaotic beginnings. Only for them to fall from power when they were over-thrown and locked away in Tartaros, behind iron gates. These being the iron gates to hell. This allowed Cronus to take possession of the sky, of time and of space and evil took control and ruled."

"The chaotic forces that created the iron gates are forever eternal and cannot be destroyed, but the portal that can connect them with the upper realm can be. Locking the gates shut once more."

"There are five principal figures associated with the prediction," he explained.

"Ophioneus- symbolising Mercury."

"Eurynome- symbolising Venus."

"Echidna- symbolising Mars."

"Calirrhoe- symbolising Jupiter."

"Chthonie- symbolising Saturn. All representing the five known planets of that time.

"They were doomed by Cronus who sent them straight to the gates of Tartaros and into hell. Where they were left for all eternity to be forgotten. In their suffering they lost sight of good and started to turn evil.

"Cronus was to be eventually killed by his son Zeus with the aid of his younger siblings, but the five figures imprisoned in hell were unaware of this. Possessed by pure evil; their human forms morphed, changing to become hell's hounds. Hideous beasts driven by the need for revenge.

"His prediction talked about a time in the distant future when the five planets would align and the iron gates to hell would be opened once more. Imprisoned for so long, hell's hounds will rise to inflict their revenge on the upper realm and on Cronus himself for vanquishing them."

He stopped to look above his head and pointed at the planets aligning as they floated above them. "Just as Zeus had managed to defeat his father with the help of his younger siblings. So too will two sibling brothers rise, to defend the upper realm. Sending the beasts back to the depths where the gates of Tartaros will be shut to retain them once more."

John looked up at the high priest. "You have a question my brother?"

"Yes master, I'm confused by your teaching. Cronus was already dead, killed by his son Zeus. Yet the five figures look to wreak revenge on the world above and on Cronus himself. Why would they reap revenge when they realise Cronus is dead. There would be no need to take revenge on the upper realm any longer?"

"They were caught by distraction, the eighth deadly sin, brother John. Allowing Cronus to trap them, aided by early humankind, and in doing they were betrayed. Eventually their betrayal turned to frustration, frustration turned to anger, anger turned to hate, and hate turned to evil and from there, there was no way back for them. All they now know is seeking revenge on the upper realm whether Cronus is alive or dead.

"When Zeus was eventually killed, another being came into force, the son of Orpheus and Eurydice. Orpheus in Greek mythology gained access to the underworld to try and reclaim his dead wife Eurydice. But was killed as they got close to the upper surface when he turned to make sure she was still following him."

"They secretly had a son however, a sorcerer who then took control. He decided to try and bring some balance back to the cosmos. But when he headed down to the gates of Tartarus to check on them, he was bitten by one of the beasts. Subsequently he became deformed, part human, part beast. He tried to purify his bloodline by producing his own siblings with another pure blood. In doing so twins came to be, one evil... one good to provide uniformity and balance once more. Only one had become the devil who decided to overthrow and kill its younger twin, then the sorcerer in a bid for evil to rule once more."

Jack now had query, "Why do you think the philosopher was talking about us?"

"It is further written in Pherecydes's prediction, that the two brothers will be cursed. One with the ability to kill the other, without the power to stop himself and the other. Forced to kill his brother to be able to destroy the devil or face being destroyed himself. He writes further that to save themselves, one must make the ultimate sacrifice, so the other can prevail."

He then turned the large book around to show them the emblem drawn back in ancient times. It was a crudely drawn triangle with a dot in the middle. "The gates to Tartaros, we know them of course as the portal gates to hell."

Jack looked up. "Master, I know that picture. Leila showed me it previously."

The high priest nodded in recognition. "The portal to the gates of hell will be in the centre of the largest warehouse and will be heavily guarded by demons. You must both enter together, that way the demons won't harm you. With the devil's servant and the hunter together, the devil will not know, what to do and will grant you passage until your intent is fully understood. Hunter your crossbow aim is off, the devil knew what to do when you were shot and has affected your good eye as a result."

"You must get up close to it to hit your target, once there, you have one shot. When you can hear the gates opening and the beasts making their way up, wait until you see the devil following. Shoot Christ's nail when you have good sight of your target and hit the devil's heart. Then throw vials of holy water into the portal. The holy water will reseal the gates, preventing the beasts from escaping and the devil will be destroyed. Allowing for the second coming to happen when peace will come to the universe once again."

Their concentration was suddenly broken by a strange vibration from above. It was the five planets floating in the illusion of the cosmos above them. They were in their final alignment phases and the best time to strike would be within the next few days.

The high priest spoke further.

"A warning to you both," raising both hands slightly.

"Brother John, you are now at the time of turning, when the

planets fully align, nothing will be able to stop that from happening. Jack, if he transforms into the devil's servant before you reach the portal, you will be faced with an impossible choice."

"He will place himself between yourself and devil to protect it. You will have to kill him to get to the devil or he will try and kill you. Either way, your curse makes your situation untenable. If, he does not turn before you get to the portal, then he will have to keep the demons at bay long enough for you to take your shot. One of you will have to make the ultimate sacrifice to save the other and all humankind."

"Is there no other way?" asked Jack.

"That has always been the way, the curse as laid down by the devil for its servant and the curse as laid down by the sorcerer for the hunter."

"But my teachings master, in your chambers… time… the universe… bending the very fabric of space and time itself. There is another way surely?"

"What we discussed is only for the ears of the hunter, not for the servant but know this, my apprentice. Time has no boundaries and time waits for no-one… It has no beginning and has no end… it has a past, and it has future. If you fail, time is where you will find the answer. This is the only remaining advice I can give you."

Chapter 16

5 August 2020
Brothers in Arms

Following the teaching session in the Golden Chamber, the third day started well before sunrise. Jack was already meditating, sitting on the rocks near the training grounds. The cold sea spray splashing onto him from below. A storm was gathering, and the sea was choppy and unwelcoming. They'd have to wait till low tide now to walk the causeway back as travelling by boat would be too dangerous.

John was with the high priest again in the Golden Chamber and the floor compasses channels were already full of liquid. Flowing straight from the cauldron as it caught the tears streaming down the statues body. The guardians had also laid out dozens of round vials and younger disciples were busy dropping them into the liquid to fill them up.

All the time the sounds above their heads were getting louder. The planets continued to move in the floating cosmos high above them. Groaning loudly as gravitational fields acted against them to pull them into alignment.

The John and the high priest were busy attaching the vials to different belts. Some to be worn around the waist, others to be hung crisscrossed over the shoulders. Both brothers had the same types of belts, but John had the most vials. He would lay down cover for Jack, while he focused on taking his shot. Jack's belts had the eight vials needed to open the portal doors and give passage back to the Chamber as well as the vials needed to close the devil's portal.

Guardians started to gather and just as before, removed their robes to reveal their battle clothes. After bowing to the high priest, they took their positions and knelt at each of the compass points. Facing the adjacent black portal doors in readiness to give final prayers for the two brothers in arms.

The high priest however was yet to take his position and lead the prayers. Instead choosing to spend his time checking everything twice over. This time the preparations had to be right, this would be their last chance to defeat the devil. Jack was now outside the chamber, but as the hunter, wasn't allowed access unless the high priest was with him. Instead of pacing around, he chose to visit the library instead. As he entered, he saw a book he had never seen before laying open on a chair. He looked around to see if anyone was there but could only here the sound of someone running down one of the corridors.

He was intrigued as he picked it up, looking to find where it belonged on the shelves. It was very old and large, a book on family trees and their blood lines. Running his finger down the index, he found a reference to his birth name Johnson and opened it on the relevant page. He could see a blood line going way back through the ages. The names of himself and John, his parents, grandparents, great grandparents and so on. Until it broke around twelve generations back where the family name Skye appeared.

This went even further back, splitting again as it went further back through the mists of time. Eventually leading to a family in Wurzburg Germany in the seventeenth century. He tried to make out their names, but they were smudged and almost illegible. Straining his eyes to try and work them out, he was suddenly distracted by the high priest walking in.

"Be careful what you read, my son, the past tends to come back to haunt if you are reckless. In the wrong hands the information the book possess could be used to destroy you. Where did you find it?"

"It was on this chair already open, master."

"This is concerning, someone has been prying and found something out about you. We must move quickly, come with me to my chambers, I must discuss something with you in private before we enter the Golden Chamber for the final blessings. The book being found changes everything and we must now be ready for all possible eventualities. I need to show you how to use time to its full advantage if things go wrong."

John was still busy in the Golden Chamber unaware of events unfolding outside. The holy water belts and some new fighting sticks for Jack, were put in the keeper's sack. The crossbow and final nail were then laid next to it, ready for the journey ahead.

A staff was banged on the ground by one the chamber guardians and the grand doors opened to allow the high priest and Jack in. He now took his position in the centre of the compass and the two brothers moved forwards to kneel at its edge. Jack grabbing the crossbow and nail just before kneeling, resting them next to him, to make sure they never left his sights again.

"My brothers we see ourselves preparing once more for a great battle. The two brave souls before you, will stand before the gates of hell. In a bid to cleanse and rid the earth of the pure evil that now surrounds it."

"Our purpose as portal guardians, to aid them when a doorway opens, but beware brothers, the forces that will be encountered will far out way what we saw before. We will be

213

staring straight into the bowels of hell itself and the beasts that lurk within. My brothers, there is a further task I must ask of you now your blood line has being discovered."

The pool of souls must be destroyed when you seal the portal. If Christ's final nail does not hit its target, it will be the fail-safe. Without the pool, the devil and it's beasts cannot feed and will die. This will also be another means of breaking your curse."

"Today mark's a special day, after millennia of battling, evil could be finally overpowered and the second coming can begin. Bringing with it peace and balance to the universe once more. Now gather your things, keeper and hunter, take our blessings with you and God speed." The pair stood to gather their things as the high priest spoke again. "One last word, hunter, remember your teachings and what was discussed, time is not your enemy, do not be afraid to use it."

A staff was banged the stone floor once more and the grand doors were opened to let the brothers out. Monks bowed their heads as the pair walked past, making their way through the corridors and up towards the church above. From there they headed across the causeway to the mainland. The wind and rain savage as they walked. Stinging their faces as they walked and thought against the strong winds. Making their way to where Jack's Range Rover was stored, they loaded up headed off for the long drive ahead.

Jack knew the warehouses like the back of his hand, following the research he'd undertaken prior to the auction. Feeding all he knew about them to his brother as they drove along. John then advising he had more holy water than Jack, as his primary role was to keep him shielded while he focused on his target. He would throw vials down as they made their way along, forming a continuous wall of holy water either side of them. The demons wouldn't then be able to attack and would buy enough time to get to the portal and fire Christ's curse to the devil's heart. Jack also had the larger vials that needed to be thrown into the portal.

The holy water would neutralise the blueish liquid in the pool. Destroying the harvested souls stored inside in the process. He felt uneasy that so many souls would be lost, but accepted it was better for them to be eradicated rather than be kept as fodder.

The last hour of travelling was sat in silence, just the sound of the radio playing to break up the quietness. In his mind John was worried he was now too far from the safety and protection of the monks and the mount. He could be overwhelmed at any time, with the yearning to transform into the devil's servant. He'd then try and kill Jack before they could fulfil their destiny. Jack was also just as worried, pondering the same thoughts in his own mind.

Eventually, they pulled in off the main street and into the alleyway where he'd last battled the devil. The place where he saw his beloved Leila shot and killed in the main courtyard between the warehouses. John as the keeper unloaded the car and lifted the contents out of the sack. The pair helped each other put their belts on as the glass vials gently clanged. The precious parcels lightly knocking together as the shoulder belts were squeezed over their heads.

Jack joked to calm their nerves, "No leather coat or hat this time, John?"

John then responding, "I still say Van Helsing would've rocked them better than you did brother. You haven't got the bum for it," smiling at him as he walked to the front of the Range Rover. Jack grinned as he tried to look behind to take a better

215

look, but all he could see were vials of water hanging below his waist. They headed down to where the energy bubble was separating the two realms and stared at the haze beyond.

Jack pushed through the energy force, entering the devil's realm first to fight off any demon's that may be waiting but it was eerily quiet. John was struggling to push through and just like before, the bubble bent inwards then deflected again. "Push harder," said Jack and as he did, his hands and arms disappeared for a second before reappearing in the realm. He stood looking at them from the other side, his eyes wide open almost in amazement as Jack grabbed them and pulled the rest of him through.

The pair carefully headed to the entrance doors of the bigger warehouse and stopped. Something felt odd, there were still no demons on guard, anywhere which worried them. Jack attached his crossbow to his chest, two special clips that had been put into his jacket just in case they had to fight their way in as he didn't want to put it down and lose it.

"Shall we knock?" whispered John, smiling, trying to hide his nerves.

"Now you come with the funny stuff," Jack replied. "No John let's just… waaaaait." It was too late, the door swung open inwards, banging loudly on the wall inside. John had pushed it as hard as he could, and the noise rattled through the empty warehouse acknowledging their arrival.

"Ok… let's not then," said Jack, shaking his head at him as they walked in.

It was almost pitch-black inside as slowly dozens and dozens of pairs of red and yellow eyes began to appear. Blinking in the darkness, then noises like hyenas communicating softly could be heard. Eyes then quickly moving from one spot to another.

Jack looked at John and whispered, "looks like we've found them then…ready?"

John whispered back, "Ready… lock and load."

Jack gently checked his crossbow was secure before reaching behind his shoulders. Pulling his fighting sticks from where they were strapped on his back. Holding them by his sides he nodded, and the pair moved forwards. They trod on slowly, straining their eyes in the darkness, as more and more pairs of eyes started to blink in the gloom.

The demons weren't sure what to do, instead hissed loudly as they walked past the first group. Either side of them more pairs of eyes peered out from behind steel columns, watching. John stood tall with a vial of holy water in each hand while Jack walked ahead slightly crouched. A vial suddenly came loose from John's belt and smashed on the floor. Causing the water to bubble and steam as it evaporated, making the demons hiss loudly. The sounds of hissing then getting much worse along with the hyena noises, as the demons started to slowly move in.

"I am the devil's servant," shouted John. "I bring the hunter to my master, so he can watch me take his soul." The demons hissed again as they backed away slightly.

The pair slowly continued and passed their first red door. "This one?" whispered Jack.

"No, it's nowhere near the devil's portal, we must get right to the mouth of it. There'll be another seven to choose from yet, keep moving."

They continued moving forwards and in the far distance they could see a small light swirling. "There, that's it, that's the portal, head in that direction," whispered John.

"I can't see a bloody thing," whispered Jack. "It's too dark, we need some light."

217

John put the vial's back on his belt and reached into his robe pockets. Whoosh… a smoking red light lit up; he'd ignited a hand-held flare. Holding it up so they could see what was in front of them.

"Can you see now, brother?"

"Oh… shit put it out…put it out…all I can see now are demons everywhere… there's hundreds of them… fucking hell."

The creatures had the ugliest of faces, some squatting, puffing their chests out and hissing. Others waiting to pounce while more moved in closer, hissing and snarling loudly. Dripping mucus and acid from their open mouths as they flicked their tongues out to show razor-sharp teeth. Poor mortals fallen foul of the eight deadly sins, now turned into demons by the devil itself. Doomed when it unleashed its retribution against them. Transforming them into their new forms and forced to serve the devil forever.

The pair drew closer together in a bid to make themselves look bigger against the demons but as the flare started to dim, they moved even closer. A huge demon stepped out in front of them to block their path and roared loudly. Shaking its head aggressively and spitting mucus at them.

Jack whispered as he pointed, "There's another red door over there, so there's now six left but we're not even a third of the way across the warehouse. I'm going to have to take him out… get ready with the water. We must make a corridor to guard our route… okay."

"Okay, Jack, after three then… one… two," but Jack didn't wait for three, the demon was already up to him. Dripping snots of acid from its mouth and nose as it breathed the foulest stench at his face. The creature roared, showing it wanted to fight but Jack didn't know how to react. So, he raised his fighting sticks, crossing them in front of him to show the same and tried to roar back as loudly as he could.

The creature tilted its head almost confused before roaring back even louder. In return he could do nothing more than punch it as hard as he could in the face. Causing it to sniff slightly as it twitched its nose. There was silence for a split second then it let loose its anger. Shaking its head and screeching in rage as it lifted its hands up ready to claw at him.

Thinking on his feet, he lobbed a vial of holy water into its mouth and the creature exploded. Vaporising a few demons in the process that were too close. The rest then went mad, scratching and tearing at each other to get to them and bring them down.

"Now John, NOW," shouted Jack and vials rained down on both sides of them, instantly forming a tall corridor of holy water. Trapping the demons on the other side and vaporising any that tried to get through.

"RUUUNNNN!" screamed John and the pair sprinted along the corridor, safely protected from the demons on either side. Any trapped demons in the corridor were bludgeoned by Jack's fighting sticks as he ran on. Pushing them into the water wall and vaporising them instantly. John then carrying on throwing vials ahead of them to clear a path.

John had now spent all but one of his belts, so Jack joined in to help. The demons kept on coming in waves, dozens, and dozens of them pouring in from all angles as the devil's portal got closer. They ran past three more red doors as Jack shouted back at John, "There's only three left now, we're running out of doors to open to be able to get back home."

A demon managed to reach out just before the next wall of water formed. Snipping one of Jack's belts with its sharp claws, and a whole belt of vials were lost as they exploded on the floor.

"Keep going, don't stop," shouted John as they ran on.

"We're getting close now, feel the heat coming from that thing." The portal was growing at an alarming rate. The yellowy white glow from within, swirling around anticlockwise getting faster and faster.

John suddenly started to slow down a little, shaking his head as if fighting with something in his head. "What's up John?" cried Jack as he stopped to try and help.

"Keep going don't stop for me... just keep running." Jack knew his brother was in trouble and although he wanted to help, he had to keep moving. He could see the last three red doors dead ahead, near the devil's portal. But John had slowed right down and the corridor of water behind, was now starting to fail. Demons were starting to get through and were quickly chasing up behind. He threw four more vials ahead to continue the corridor and unclipped his crossbow. Loading Christ's last nail before running again.

He past two more doors, knowing he'd be unable to get to them anymore. The corridor of water was now blocking his route, but the last door was still there, very close to the portal itself. He needed that one to make his escape and had to protect his exit. With three normal sized vials left and one needed to open their own portal door to the Golden Chamber, he had two to use against the demons. He also had the five large vials to destroy the pool of souls and seal the gates to hell again.

Stopping at the portals rim a strong vortex rushed around him, making it a struggle to stand up. Its energy forces blowing outwards, pulling up from the depths below. He could hear the shrieks and growls of creatures starting to come up from the depths, time was running out. The gates to hell were now open and the beasts were on their way. He shouted to John to hurry, but he was still struggling quite a distance back. Jack was now torn, help his brother who was probably already turning or save humankind. He had to listen to his head and not his heart and knew his brother was sacrificing himself.

He threw two more vials near himself, forming the last section of water wall to buy some more time. Leaving the last vial to open the portal door to escape. He looked back and could see the demon's closing in fast on John. He had no choice but to throw one of the large vials in a bid to try and help. It exploded way behind, and a wave of water hit, vaporising a large number instantly.

He threw his last small vial at the red door turning it black and a portal door opened to the Golden Chamber. The clock was now ticking as he looked behind again. He could see more demons closing in on John again but there was nothing more he could do. He shrieked to him to move, and he started to run again. Turning back to the devil's portal, he could hear the creatures from the lower realm getting louder and louder. The portal was getting even larger, and he was able to stand in its rim to look downwards. Below he could see a wide winding stone staircase, disappearing down into the depths and nothing but darkness below.

He threw the last of the large vials into the portal and watched them disappear into the gloom. He turned and shouted again to his brother. "Quick John… we've no time left, the chambers portal will shut soon, and we'll be trapped," but John had slowed right down, walking holding his hands held out.

"Fire the nail, Jack, fire it and save yourself, do it now, don't wait for me."

The ground began to shake beneath them as the large vials delivered their payloads. Exploding in the pit of hell below as a defining shriek was heard, the devil was coming up. "Come on

John… we've got to go, NOW." He held his crossbow up taking aim to fire, but John was in serious trouble. The floor started to break apart as demons came up, tearing and grabbing at his legs and feet, while others pulled at his robes from behind. Jack had no more weapons left to help and could only watch on in horror. Demons ripped John's robes off and flesh had started to be ripped from him as they began to drag him down.

John looked up his voice now changing and his eyes red, he was turning into the devil's servant. "Fire the bolt… Jack… do it… nooowww…. arhhhh…" in a demonic voice. As he fought to keep his mind and try and break free, he was pulled deeper into the ground, until only his flailing arms could be seen. More demons joined in, pushing, and pulling him down into the depths until with one last tug, he was gone.

Jack swung round pointing the crossbow into the devil's portal, standing in its wake. From the depths below he could see shadows making their way up. Five beastly creatures running up the stone staircase on all fours. Their shadows casting the forms of huge demonic beasts, then the shadow of something larger coming up beside them. The devil had transformed itself and was flying up screeching in anger.

Jack looked down and shouted over the noise, "LUCIFER, THIS ONES ON ME. WHAT WAS ONCE MINE IS NOW DEFINIATELY YOURS," firing true and straight at the devil's heart.

Quickly turning he could see the guardians through his own portal ready to give help. The high priest stood beckoning him to come through as it started to close. He threw the crossbow through first and stopped. Turning to glance down into the devil's portal, to make sure he'd finished the job. He could see the devil and one of the hounds falling together as it began to implode. Taking a running dive he made his escape, just as the devil's own portal imploded on itself.

Chapter 17

Retribution

He jolted heavily taking a huge breath as though for the first time and sat bolt upright in his hospital bed. Pulling the tubes from his mouth and throat, coughing, and gagging heavily in the process. He then pulled out the drips and sensors that were attached to the machines monitoring him. He'd come out of his coma and was becoming alert as he looked around his surroundings.

Nurses hearing the alarms from the machines as he disconnected himself, burst in thinking it was an emergency. Only to be left baffled how he was suddenly awake. He could talk, he could use his hands and arms, he could move his legs and feet and when the bandages were removed from around his head, the wound had all but healed.

He couldn't understand what was going on, he was in the same bed, the same room with the same nurses and doctors all as before. "Are you okay, can you hear us all right?" asked a doctor.

"Yes, I can hear you fine where am I?"

"You're in hospital, you've been in a coma after you were shot in the head."

"That must mean everything I've experienced since the courtyard has been nothing more than a dream. It's all been in my head; I need to get back to the mount as soon as possible."

"You'll need to give a statement to the police, Mr Skye, they need to know what happened in the courtyard where you were found."

"That's going to be difficult to explain, can you put them off for now at all?"

"Of course," said a nurse. "We'll let them know that you're now conscious but still too weak to give a statement at present." She smiled and left the room closely followed by the others. Jack laid his head back on the pillows. His head was thumping, and his ears ringing and quickly fell back to sleep.

Twenty-four hours past and although he was still feeling stiff and sore, he was able to walk around his room. Albeit a little unstable at first on his legs. The glass in the windows was opaque and there was no way of opening them. So, he couldn't see out or let any fresh air in. The room itself was clean and comfortable but smelt strongly of disinfectant. Some fresh clothes were laid out on a chair near the washbasin and behind the curtain was a toilet and shower.

He checked his watch to see what the time was, but it had stopped working. The face had a large crack across it and the time was stuck on 11.47 p.m. on 12 July. He shook his wrist before tapping the watches face but it was broken, stuck on the exact time he got shot in the head.

He felt his neck and his necklace was still there, but he had no way of telling if it still had any power or not. In his dream it saved his life but didn't have enough reserve to complete his healing. The high priest then intervening by entering his mind kinetically to reconnect his body with his mind. Then using the healing stone at the mount to finish the healing process.

He got dressed, sat on the edge of the bed mulled over what he'd say to the police. Also wondering where John and the monks were. The door opened, and another doctor and nurse walked in to do some tests.

"How are you feeling today, Jack, isn't it?" asked the nurse. "It's good to see you're up and about at last. You must be feeling much better." The doctor turned to him and asked if there was anything concerning him. Jack advised he was fine apart from some buzzing in his head and whistling in his ears. "That's to be expected," said the doctor. "It should subside in a few days."

"There are some friends of yours in the waiting room if you feel up to seeing them?" said the nurse. "Your brother has been here for last few days, waiting for any news, they'll all be so relieved to see you're better... how about it?"

"Sure," he said, "there's no time like the present, can you show me the way."

The nurse opened the door and made her way out. "This way Jack, if you'd like to follow me, her take my arm as well, you still look a bit wobbly." They left the room taking a slow walk down the corridor. At the end they turned right and continued to follow the overhead signs, guiding them to where the waiting rooms were.

Eventually they came to a door saying 'Waiting Room 1' where the nurse stopped. "This is your stop then Jack. Your friends and brother are waiting for you on the other side. They'll be so pleased, they've been dying to see you," smiling strangely at him. "I'll check on you in a bit." Smiling at him again as she walked off, disappearing around another corner.

He gripped the handle and with a slight push, opened the door and walked through. He greeted by a strange landscape, there was no waiting room and there was no-one there to meet him. Instead, he was faced a landscape that weirdly expanded outwards as he stepped on it. The scene was sparse, almost barren and the natural light had a strange darkness to it. The air was hot and dank and the land in front of him shimmered in the heat. The only noises he could hear were like fires raging.

In the distance he could see a shape or some form of structure and headed towards it. Initially he couldn't work out what it was due to the shimmering haze until he got closer. He could just make out what looked like some sort of throne. Purposely set on top of a four-sided pyramid with stairs running up each side. He could also make out some shapes moving around the bottom of it and saw five beasts tethered at the bottom.

They growled menacingly as he stood before them, pulling at their tethers to get at him. "Easy my beauties… Ophioneus, Eurynome, Echidna, Calirrhoe, Chthonie… steady." Came a voice from behind the structure. They continued snarling and grumbling as they slowly settled again. Turning in circles before laying down, with one licking at one of its giant front paws. Jack knew the voice all too well. He stood ready to fight, as a beastly figure slid round tight to the throne, transforming into its human form.

"Hi, Jackee, how yah doing?"

"Lucifer, how the hell did you survive?"

"Who said I survived, who said you survived," he then shouted out on the top of his voice, "Who said the world survived?" Spreading his arms up above his head and laughing as he danced around, circling in a mocking manner.

"You're the devil… I killed you… I destroyed this realm and everything in it."

"Did you, Jackee boy? did you really? all you managed to destroy was the pool of souls and re-sealed the portal. We'll make another pool and another portal soon enough. You see the planets are still aligned and it's our time."

"Where am I, Lucifer, why didn't you die?"

"Questions… questions… questions… always questions

with you. You managed to destroy the portal, sealing us down here but as you tried to make your escape. The portal expanded before imploding on itself, sucking you in before you could reach the safety of your own. The hospital set up was just a ruse my way of mocking you. Welcoming you to hell with a false sense of security." He smiled in an antagonising manner, tilting his head to one side slightly.

"Oh… that reminds me… someone's waiting to say hello." He walked in front of the beasts and stared hard at them. "Ophioneus, Eurynome, Echidna, Calirrhoe, Chthonie if you'd be so kind."

The beasts stood up and pulled at their tethers, slowly turning the structure round so the front of the throne was on full view. From high above a beast swooped down, landing at the bottom. Slowly making its way up the stone stairs, it began transforming. Finally turning into its true human form as it sat on the throne.

"Jack, it's so nice to see you again… have you missed me… I've missed you?"

"Leila… it can't be… you're dead, you were killed by the devil himself, I saw Lucifer shoot you."

She laughed, "Oh… Jack, typical man, only seeing what your eyes and mind want you to. I amm the devil and now you along with your brother belong to me." Pointing to her left and a barren open area. A crucifix had been set up and nailed to it, was John, with demons ripping and tearing at his legs and feet. He manged to look up, his eyes red and evil looking. In a demonic voice he howled and pleaded for his brother to save him.

Jack fell onto his hands and knees, unable to stand any longer and looked at the ground feeling nauseous. "Oh… Jack, you don't need to beg to me, at least not yet anyway."

He shook his head in disbelief, "How…how did this happen?"

"Well, you see, here's the thing Jack. Lucifer's just a name synonymous with the devil, and as such over the millennia, my servants have always been given it. It makes for a great disguise, no one ever expects the devil to be a woman."

"The Lucifer, you see, standing before you, has been the best and longest serving one yet. He's collected hundreds and hundreds of souls and has grown to really love his job. His service to me was extended as your brother was kept protected from me for years. But now he can pay his debt to me in full. He'll suffer torment before I fully complete his transformation to become my servant."

She turned to Lucifer, "Stand before me."

Lucifer did as commanded and stood at the bottom step, bowing his head. "Master?"

"John William James, your duty to me is complete. You can now be released from my service your curse is lifted."

Lucifer transformed into a simple looking farm worker as Jack looked on in astonishment. "You, now have a choice, you can be transported back to your old life and re-join your young family. Having no recollection of me at all or you can stay here in the modern world. With all the wealth and knowledge, you've gleaned over the years. Continue to reap chaos but without the special powers I gave to you."

A rather soft voice spoke, "I…I… I would like to go back to my old life, be with my wife and children again and watch them grow up."

It suddenly all made sense, Jack remembered Lucifer's words in his office. Where he said he'd tried to be a family man many… many years previously, before being pulled in a different direction. He didn't walk away from his relationship at all, he simply didn't become the devil's servant until he was in his early twenties. By which time he was already married with young children.

Leila looked most put out. "As you wish," flicking her right hand dismissively.

He then held his hands up to stop her. "Wait I have one more request to make, as a thank-you for the extra service I've given to you."

"What is it… speak?"

"My sister… I want her to come back to me."

"That's not possible, she was a devil hunter, and you took her soul when you transformed. You gave her life force to me to feed on… I cannot return that."

Again, Jack realised the importance of the skull he appeared to mourn in his office. It was his sister's skull he'd kept it with him as a reminder of what he'd done to her.

"Now you must return what was once given to you."

She walked down the stairs from her throne, holding out a hand. He removed his ring and gave it to her, from his labourer's jacket he pulled out the fist of God whip. Leila held it up in the shimmering haze.

"Ah, yes… father's fist and wrist. A weak being neither beast nor human. Even when we dug up his skeleton, he looked pathetic. I just wish I'd hidden the scrolls and earthenware somewhere safer. The story of how I came to be and how I destroyed my twin and father was never supposed to be recorded.

"If you were wiser, Jack, you would've worked it all out just like Reg had. He had to be removed before he could tell you who I really was." She clicked her fingers making a rolled-up document appear.

"When I tear this document you, John William James, will return to your old life, never to remember this time. To carry on your life as a farmer, just as you were the day you were collected," as she went to tear it, she stopped. "Oh… I nearly forgot, you've something else that belongs to me," she pushed her fingers into his chest pulling out the nail Jack had shot him with previously. "Now you may go," And as she tore the contract, he disappeared. She sighed disappointedly, "Such a waste, he was the most fiendish ruthless servant I've ever had."

"Now to you, Jack, what do we do with you now?" turning to face him.

"Lucifer wanted to kill you, but I said you were too precious to me. After all we are betrothed, what better way to take control of your curse than by having the devil hunter serve and protect me."

"You've got no chance," answered Jack. "I'll never serve you. Become a servant of evil, I'll kill you first."

"With what," she scoffed. "My brothers poisoned nails; I already have one imbedded in me from millennia ago. This one that you hit Lucifer with, thinking he was me, and oh yes, the one you fired at me in the portal."

"I shot it straight to your heart, you should be dead."

"Yes… although you thought Lucifer was the devil, you did shoot at me. After you destroyed my pool of souls, my intention was to destroy you, then reap the full wrath of hell on the upper realm. But I hadn't realised you had the third nail, it was indeed heading straight for my heart but Ophioneus over there, jumped off the staircase to protect me and the nail hit him in his paw."

She walked over to where the beast sat licking at it. Cupping its giant paw in her hands, she pulled it out. "There… there," she said. "All better now," giving the beast a kiss on its head. "I now

230

have all three nails, Jack, and you have no more holy water, you will serve me."

"NEVER," he shouted.

"Oh… but you will, not only is your brother nailed to that cross so he can't get down he also needs further punishment. For hiding from me for so many years with the monks. Every day moving forwards, the demons will feed on him. Stripping his body clean and as he regenerates every night, so the process will start all over again. The only way to spare his punishment is for you to replace the souls you destroyed and replenish the pool once I've made a new one."

Jack quickly scoffed back, "You've no souls to feed upon, you'll die in days and the curse will be broken. My brother's punishment will be short lived."

The devil sneered back again. "The high priest's teachings serve you well, but you underestimate me. I have a soul that will keep me going for a little while yet."

"Suck my soul out and you'll have no one to gather others for you," he replied.

"Oh, I have no intention of feeding on your soul, Jack, I'll have a new one every day to feed on. When your brother regenerates, either replenish the pool or sit and watch for the next thirty years as I suck the shear life out of him daily… YOUR MOVE, JACK."

He stood for a short while then sat, folding his legs into a half lotus position and began to meditate. There was a thud as something landed next to him. He opened an eye and saw the fist of God whip lying next to him, then heard the chink of a ring hitting against rock as it bounced.

"Take these things and fulfil your destiny in joining me. You know what my father's fist does… as for the ring… when we were in France you asked if the ring, I gave you had the power of transportation. I said no but one existed but hadn't been found, well I lied. I've owned it for a very long time and previous Lucifer's have used it to transport themselves from place to place."

Jack recalled in his mind again how Lucifer had simply disappeared in his office that day. How he'd also suddenly appeared and disappeared on the CCTV footage at the conference centre fire. He now realised how Lucifer could get around so easily.

"I won't serve you, Leila, but I will kill you. In the fullness of time, I will somehow kill you. Time is endless and I can wait," He threw the items back at her.

"Your teachings will not help you here, your priest forgets that time has no relevance. I can travel forwards or backwards in it to suit myself. Perhaps even seek out your own bloodline and eradicate them, you would then fail to exist. Yes, I'm fully aware of your bloodline and where it started, your high priest has a mole in his camp."

"Only you can't leave here now, can you," replied Jack. "You're trapped the portal has been destroyed and hells gates sealed. You'll have to wait another thousand years to get the chance to open it again. By the time that happens you'll already be dead, my brother's soul won't sustain you for that long and neither would mine."

The devil clicked her fingers again and a contract appeared. "Dear Jack… I'm afraid we've a contract and under its terms, I refer to a clause. A clause added by your very own lawyer I believe, one which you've broken." Jack had finally had enough of her games and made it quite clear the only contract he'd signed was with Lucifer and not her.

"You, silly fool, Lucifer was only the MD of the company, I'm the CEO. If you'd read the terms properly you would've noticed, he was signing on my behalf. You've broken the contract and I'm now calling in the debt in full."

She read the clause that Reg had insisted went in to protect him.

"The contracted agreement may be terminated by either party, at any time, now or in the future. At any point of the said agreement being breached by either party as further caveated. This being any wrongdoing undertaken or implemented by either party, will be fully compensated in full by the offender. To the offended, within a timescale that is to be agreed by the said offended party. That being that the other party has/ was/ being unlawfully wronged by the other."

"I won't play your games, Leila, you're wasting your time." He sat down again ignoring her and prepared to meditate again.

"You tried to double-cross me by entering into a separate agreement with another consortium. You didn't have my written permission and you purposely made sure I would lose on the bidding. Furthermore, you've committed all the deadly sins including the eighth. Your already on a path leading straight to evil, the same path you trod years ago as a young adult."

"I want compensation for your actions you owe me. You'll gather souls for me until I'm satisfied the debt has been fully repaid. Your brother will continue being punished until such time I feel his debt is also repaid, then you'll be my slave and protector forevermore. Ensuring no more hunters can be generated while you're still live. Part of the curse I bet your precious high priest even overlooked. I'll leave you with those thoughts while I start to find a way out of here. In the meantime, you can sit and watch your brother suffer, until you come to your senses and do as I

233

ask."

"I WILL HAVE RETRIBUTION," she screamed in a hideous voice, before transforming into a beast again and flying off.

John managed to look up from his cross and called to Jack in his demonic voice. "Brother… just agree to get the souls… don't do this… help me."

Jack remained calm and controlled, he knew the devil would quickly weaken, he also now fully understood the high priest's cryptic advice. Time was the key, the words ringing in his ears. Time has no boundaries and time waits for no-one… It has no beginning and has no end… it has a past, and it has future. If you fail, time is where you will find the answer.

John shouted across again as demons slowly started to move in to start feeding, "BROTHER HELP MEeeee."

Jack remained sitting, blocking his mind from the situation. Choosing instead to fall into a deep meditative trance, focusing purely on the cosmos. His mind drifted as he imagined himself floating through time and space, travelling past the planets and out to the furthest reaches of the universe. Travelling faster and faster, his mind unlocking other galaxies and planets. He continued heading towards the centre of creation itself, to the place where nothing existed before the big bang.

He meditated for what felt like a few hours, only to realise when he opened his eyes again that days had now flown by. His necklace was somehow glowing bright once more, busily sustaining him, but it was a different story for the beasts. They were curled up, weak and dying, as they had no souls to feed on. He looked around but there was no sign of the devil, only the body of a monk lying on the ground. Then he heard laughter, it was John speaking in his demonic voice again.

"You'll not find my master, she's gone from this place, the monk you see dead before you, a spy from the monastery. He managed to open a one-way portal to escape. Using an artefact given to him prior to him being placed in the monastery. He arrived before you did and divulged what he saw in that book. His reward for being so loyal, she took his soul out and fed on it to keep herself alive."

"Where is she now, brother?"

John hissed, "Don't call me brother, you let me suffer in this way and do nothing to help."

"I will help you, John, if you help me… where is she?"

"The monk's soul gave her enough power to use Lucifer's ring, after putting it on she gave it a twist and vanished."

"That's not the whole story is it, where's she gone John?"

John laughed as his demonic side took over again, "She's gone into hiding until she fully recovers. She's going to track our bloodline back and destroy our forefathers. You will never leave this place and soon you will never have existed. Your trapped here and she will destroy you."

"So… she's weak and wanting revenge against me. That makes more vulnerable and dangerous than I realised. This has to end now; the second coming must be allowed to happen."

He took off his jacket and ripped the lining open. Pulling out a small mirror and placed it against some rocks. He stared at it intensely, opening his mind and his reflection started to wobble. A small section of John's room could be seen in the monastery, but the opening was too small to be able to get through.

John laughed at his attempt to escape, but quickly stopped as Jack leaned forwards. Touching the outside of it, he slowly moving his fingers sideways, then upwards. Making the hole bigger until it was large enough for him to crawl through.

John screamed again for him not to leave him. But Jack knew if he freed him, he'd try and kill him to protect his master. "I'm sorry, John, I can't help right now, I must find her and finish this. Time waits for no man but that's where I'll find the devil, hiding in the past. I will return for you I promise."

Crouching down he shuffled his way through on his hands and knees. Then jumped down from the ledge that had formed in John's room. Running to his desk he grabbed a vial of holy water and threw it at the shimmering portal. John could be heard screaming on the other side as demon's moved in to feast on him again, then it sealed shut. Sitting on John's bed to take in what had happened, the high priest walked in.

"Did you succeed?"

"You were right to make me take the mirror as a fail-safe. The portal imploded on itself, and I was sucked in and trapped in hell. John is being punished for hiding for so many years, he's on a crucifix like Christ. He's half turned but until his punishment has been completed, he is being made to suffer."

"He sacrificed himself to give you time to take your shot. Just as the predication was made in the ancient text. What about the devil and its beasts, were they destroyed?"

"The gates to hell are sealed again, the beasts of hell are dying, and the pool of souls was destroyed. The devil still prevails and managed to escape. It gets worse, Leila is the devil and has been using deception on me the whole time. She's killed one of the monks and managed to get enough energy from his soul to escape using Lucifer's ring. She's gone into hiding to recover and used her dark powers to take her back in time."

"The monk you talk about was a spy, he is the one who left the book on the chair in the library. Looking at your family's bloodline to find where it began. He escaped just before we could stop him, he killed and injured many of our brothers in the process. They are trying to clear the mess up still now; the devil will now know your full bloodline and where it began."

"She won't know completely though master, the name at the bottom. It couldn't be read but I think I know where she'll be heading." The high priest was confused but refrained from comment. Jack clearly had other things on his mind as he quickly left the room.

He followed as he made his way to the armoury to collect his crossbow and carried on until they reached the Golden Chamber. "I need to be let in master, grant me access." Without asking questions he banged the door with his staff and the doors opened. The guardians on duty bowed their heads then quickly left, to stand on guard outside.

"There," said Jack, pointing at a small rectangular shape cut into the centre point of the floors compass. "Where you stood before in, battle that shape, it's cut out to take an object. Where's the Antikythera Mechanism."

The high priest walked up the stairs to the altar and fetched it from a hidden shelf behind. "This doesn't just predict the movement of the planets, does it, it does more," as he looked above his head at the floating cosmos. "It lets you play with time and space itself... doesn't it?"

"Your instinct serves you well, hunter. The device allows you to travel back into the past, but only within your own lifetime. You can go backwards but you cannot go further forwards, as the unwritten future does not yet exist... there are also risks involved... to travel back in time you must bend the fabric of time and space itself."

He drew a circle on the floor with a line running vertically through the middle of it. He explained the line represented a person's timeline, from birth through to death. With the two halves of the circle representing separate things. The first a person's life span, from their birth through to their death. The second being death back to birth, a complete circle of life.

Using this theory, he explained Jack would be able to follow the same curve, by bending and distorting space and time. Allowing him to go backwards and visit a point during his own lifetime that had already occurred. He warned that he could not interfere with what had happened in his past, however. Otherwise, his present could then fail to exist as a result, along with him.

He also warned about trying to return to the present. "Time will have moved on and what was your present, right here, right now, will be the past. The real present will now be in the future, is this clear?"

Jack nodded as he continued, "To travel back to the present, you will have to make your way up the other curve, the timeline from your birth. To do this you will have to distort time and space even further... do you understand?"

"Yes, master... but you said the future doesn't exist yet in time?"

He pointed to the sketch on the floor again with his staff. "The two curves also represent two people that have a connection. There will be two of you in the past, you must not let your younger self see who you are. He does not know his destiny yet. Your past is what defined you and you cannot interfere with it. Time is the key to your question however and time will help you work out how to best use it."

"I need to go somewhere where I can find help in getting even further back into the past. Not decades but centuries, the devil will be hiding in my ancestor's past, I need to follow."

The high priest held up his hands in caution. "To go back that far is a journey no-one has ever attempted. Even if you succeed in getting there, to come back would be nigh on impossible. It is an unwritten, unproven law, time would have moved on, you will have to travel even further to catch it back up. It will likely end with you being trapped in the past for the rest of your life."

"There's no choice I have to go back and finish what has started, the devil is vulnerable. I must flush it out and destroy it, to save humanity and break the curse. Perhaps it's me that's to make the ultimate sacrifice and not John?"

"My son, the same laws will apply to the devil. There will be two of them now and it will have no problem in sharing its identity with the other to protect itself. To go back you will need to kill the younger version so the one from this time will never have existed and there it will end. How do you plan to kill it, you have no crucifix nails, only the crossbow?"

"Where I'm planning to go all three will be there, that's my destiny—now show me how the device operates."

The high priest placed the Antikythera Mechanism in the cut out and the box opened. Unfolding its sides to reveal the main cogs and workings inside. Jack looked at the different coloured cogs and asked how to make the mechanism work.

"When I set the mechanism in motion, you must concentrate on a time, place, and a date to go to. The green dials there, turn them all the way to the left, this will set them ready to engage. Each cog and notch refers to a day, a week, and a month in the calendar… but remember, when I ask you to think about the date the ancient Greeks used thirteen calendar months, so choose your thoughts wisely."

Jack did as asked and turned all the dials to the left setting them ready to start.

"Now the amber dials, turn all these to the right… this will set the time and year that you will provide."

Again, Jack did as he asked and set the cogs turning them all the way to the right. "Finally, the red dials, push them all the way down so they fold back into themselves, this will set the place you will be going to when you choose it."

As he pushed, they slowly pulled together, dropping inside one another to form a small pyramid shape. As he stood up, he looked down at the box. It was now twice its original size and appeared to have many different layers and depths to it. Almost like looking into the workings of a high precision watch. The high priest guided him to the altar where two belts of holy water were stored behind it, along with a new set of fighting sticks.

Jack smiled as if he must have already known what he wanted. Having them prepared in advance, ready for his next journey. The priest helped him put the belts on, then Jack stowed his fighting sticks behind his back and clipped his crossbow to his replaced jacket. He was then led him back to the middle of the compass to stand next to the box.

"Good luck on your journey, hunter, the devil must be stopped before it finds the start of your bloodline. If it does and your ancestor is destroyed, you will never have existed. The devil would then be able to realise the hounds, as the portal would not have been destroyed." He then pushed the end of his staff into the centre of the small pyramid and started the mechanism.

An ellipse arose from the groves surrounding the centre of the compass and enveloping Jack in the process. Jack was amazed, with himself standing in the middle, it formed the same sketch that the high priest had drawn on the floor. It started to slowly spin, making a whoomph sound as each segment completed a rotation. At first, he could see the stars in the cosmos in front of him, before they quickened. Stars stretching out to form lines like a time lapse photograph of the night sky. The ellipse spun faster and faster, making louder and quicker whoomph sounds as it sped up, whoomph, whoomph, whoomph, whoomph.

He thought about the day before he left for France, when he was escaping his old life. In his mind he set the time, date, and place he wanted to go back to as a tunnel began to form in front of him. Bending and twisting, spreading out into the distance like a large worm hole forming. Connecting itself to a point in the past and providing him a passageway to travel along.

Strong winds rushed around his face and body, making his jacket and hair flap wildly as he shouted, "I PROMISED JOHN I'D RETURN FOR HIM. I WILL FULFILL MY PROMISE AND I'LL SEE YOU IN THE FUTURES PRESENT." He stood staring into the worm hole and the darkness of space surrounding it. With one final look around the chamber then a quick glance at the high priest, he dived in and was gone. The ellipse dropped, and the Antikythera Mechanism closed itself up again. Forming its rectangular shape as its sides folded back into place.

"Good luck hunter," said the high priest as he picked it back up and walked back to the altar. Stopping midway, he turned to stare at the statue. Noticing a single tear drop run down one of its cheeks. He watched on as it continued down it's body and into the cauldron. "Hmmm," he said to himself as he placed the mechanism back behind the altar. Standing for a moment by the altar, he looked up at the floating cosmos, then back the statue again before walking out. As the portal guardians returned to their sentry duties inside. He put his hands behind his back and wandered off down the corridor, deep in contemplation.